The Second Story

The MAGIC MISFITS

The Second Story

By Neil Patrick Harris
& Alec Azam

STORY ARTISTRY BY LISSY MARLIN
HOW-TO MAGIC ART BY KYLE HILTON

Little, Brown and Company
New York Boston

Text and illustrations copyright © 2018 by Neil Patrick Harris.

Story illustrations by Lissy Marlin. How-To illustrations by Kyle Hilton.

Cover art by Lissy Marlin. Cover design by Karina Granda.
Cover art copyright © 2018 by Neil Patrick Harris.
Cover copyright © 2018 by Hachette Book Group, Inc.

Little, Brown and Company
Hachette Book Group
1290 Avenue of the Americas, New York, NY 10104
Visit us at LBYR.com

First Edition: September 2018

Little, Brown and Company is a division of Hachette Book Group, Inc.
The Little, Brown name and logo are trademarks of Hachette Book Group, Inc.

The publisher is not responsible for websites (or their content)
that are not owned by the publisher.

Library of Congress Cataloging-in-Publication Data
Names: Harris, Neil Patrick, 1973– author. | Azam, Alec, author. |
Marlin, Lissy, illustrator.
Title: Magic misfits : the second story / by Neil Patrick Harris & Alec Azam ;
story artistry by Lissy Marlin ; how-to magic by Kyle Hinton.
Description: First edition. | New York ; Boston : Little, Brown and Company, 2018. | Series:
Magic Misfits ; 2 | Summary: Leila and the other Magic Misfits have the opportunity to perform
with a famous stage psychic known as Madame Esmeralda, who may hold secrets to Leila's past.
Identifiers: LCCN 2017056646| ISBN 9780316391856 (hardcover : alk. paper) |
ISBN 9780316391832 (ebook : alk. paper) | ISBN 9780316391863 (library edition
ebook : alk. paper)
Subjects: | CYAC: Magic tricks—Fiction. | Orphans—Fiction. | Identity—Fiction. |
Psychics—Fiction. | Friendship—Fiction. | Gay fathers—Fiction. | Humorous stories.
Classification: LCC PZ7.1.H3747 Mam 2018 | DDC [Fic]—dc23
LC record available at https://lccn.loc.gov/2017056646

ISBNs: 978-0-316-39185-6 (hardcover), 978-0-316-39183-2 (ebook),
978-0-316-41986-4 (large print), 978-0-316-52639-5 (int'l),
978-0-316-48724-5 (B&N special edition)

Printed in the United States of America

LSC-C

10 9 8 7 6 5 4 3 2 1

To Harper and Gideon,
because the latter was listed first
in the previous book
and the former was far from pleased.

TABLE OF CONTENTS

WELCOME BACK!

Yes, *you*...the one with the awesome hair and this book in your hands!

Who else would I be talking to?

You've returned! How nice to see you again! It's been too long. If I know you at all, I'll bet you're seeking an escape from the ordinary and looking for more adventure, more puzzles, more *em-ay-gee-eye-see*. Well, look no further. I have another story to tell you.... Have I ever!

I hope you remember everything we discussed in the last book. It will make it easier to hop back in....

Need a refresher? No problem!

Let's begin with our delightful cast. Do you recall the boy with fast fingers? The orphan, **Carter Locke**, was a wiz with card tricks and could make things vanish—and reappear too! Though truthfully, he didn't believe in real magic until he hopped a train to the town of Mineral Wells, where wonders appeared around every corner—from the buzzing circus tents of the fairgrounds to the magnificent auditorium way up in the hills at the Grand Oak Resort.

His friend **Leila Vernon** was the young and bright-eyed escape artist extraordinaire, who wrangled out of handcuffs and straitjackets as easily as if she'd played with them as toys in her cradle. Surely it had nothing to do with her lucky lockpicks, given to her by her fathers, whom she lived with above a certain magic shop on Main Street.

Let us not forget **Theo Stein-Meyer**, the multitalented violin prodigy who could levitate objects using his violin bow. Yes, music can be soothing for the soul, and for the heart, especially when it comes with magic. Theo rarely showed his  regally thoughtful face around Mineral Wells unless he was dressed in one of his favorite and famous tuxedos.

 There was also our little spitfire, **Ridley Larsen**, whose mad-scientist red hair made her look just as fierce as she acted. She could transform one object into another and then back again all before you could say "*Abracadabra!*" Ridley kept a notebook hidden in a compartment in the arm of her wheelchair so she could work out puzzles and invent secret codes to share with her friends. If you're especially kind, maybe one day she'll share them with you too. (Or maybe she already has.)

And last (but not least!) were the hilarious **Izzy and Olly**, the comedic Golden twins, who performed at the

Grand Oak Resort. Those two were quite the act, both literally and figuratively. If you wanted laughs, those were the twins you needed.

In our previous tale, not long ago—*or was it forever ago? I can't remember*—Carter, Leila, Theo, Ridley, Olly, and Izzy used their stage magic skills to stop a rash of petty robberies and ultimately prevented the theft of the world's largest diamond. Working together, these six kids bonded while battling the barbaric B. B. Bosso, and thus formed a very special magic club called *the Magic Misfits*.

Is it all coming back now?

Brilliant!

Now, for another reminder...

HOW TO

Read This Book!

The volume you are currently holding tells the next chapter in the saga of our misfit magicians. Like the one that came before, this book is also filled with lessons on magic—lessons that you can practice in your bedroom or basement or school gymnasium.

If you read the whole thing, both the tale and the lessons, you'll likely come away with some skills of your own—skills that you can use to make your friends gasp and gag and giggle with gratitude. There may even be laughter and clapping. Because isn't that what this is all about: making your friends smile and giving them an *escape* from the ordinariness of the everyday?

Once again, I must ask that you keep the secrets of the magical lessons to *yourself*. In other words, please don't go whispering them into sewer grates in the dead of night. And don't stand in front of an audience and explain how each trick works before or after you perform them. It ruins the illusion, and you probably won't get the same kind of applause. And, of course, refrain from reciting the lessons to any gossips in your school. You never know when a rival magician might show up and thwart your hard work. Rival magicians can be *tricky* that way.

If you do feel the need to share these lessons, make sure it's with a group of your best friends, those who've promised to keep your secrets—a magicians' club, if you will, just like our very own Magic Misfits. After all, secret organizations are quite fun. Who doesn't want to be part of a club?

One of the most fun things to do with other magic-minded folks is to put on a show. Keep this in mind as you discover the magic lessons within these pages. How would you set your stage to impress your audience? Would you use a great red curtain? Or would you start in pitch-darkness to add a sense of mystery and tension? Would one of your friends act as an announcer? Or might your magic club begin the show in silence?

These questions are not only useful when staging

a magical production but they also come in handy when telling a story like the one I am about to begin. Personally, I feel that a mixture of the following aspects is most effective: curtains, trapdoors, shadows, mirrors, music, sound effects, voice-overs, and fog. And don't forget the sense of excitement of a new journey.

Are you ready to find out which of these I've chosen to start our show?

I mean, *story*?

Well then, go on and turn the page!

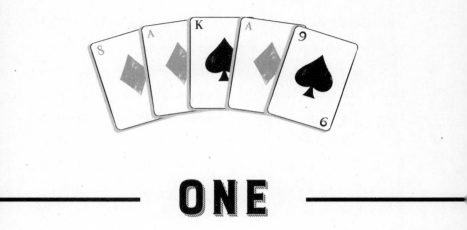

ONE

Leila Vernon did not always live in Mineral Wells. In fact, her name had not always been Leila Vernon. When she stayed at Mother Margaret's Home for Children, Leila's last name had been *Doe*.

Doe was not a name that she'd been given by family—*Doe* was Leila's name because no one knew who her family was. When Mother Margaret first found Leila, a notecard in the bassinet stated only her first name and birth date. Leila never let this get the better of her. In fact, she tried harder than the other girls to keep a positive attitude, even when they treated her as if she were as worthless as a wooden nickel.

That was why, one afternoon, when several girls from Mother Margaret's Home were dragging Leila Doe down the hallway toward Mother Margaret's office, Leila let out a loud and boisterous laugh. "Ha-ha-ha!" she shouted as they pinched her arms. "That tickles!"

Leila was not *actually* tickled by what the mean girls were doing to her, but she figured that maybe an adult would hear her loud cries and intervene. She didn't need to be psychic to know what the girls were up to, as they locked her in the darkest closet in the whole orphanage at least once a week. All because the tallest of the bunch had decided at some point that she didn't like Leila always smiling and being cheery.

The tall girl wished for Leila to be as miserable as she was. And so she and her friends went out of their way to torment Leila every chance they got. Leila fought with every breath to not show them how much they were hurting her, especially on this particular afternoon, when a group of *real-live magicians* from the town of Mineral Wells was going to perform for all the children. Leila had been looking forward to the show for weeks.

"Come on, guys!" Leila said with a forced smile. "Let's all go down to the recreation room. Everyone is probably waiting for us. There might even be cookies!"

The only response she got was a twisted echo of her last statement. *"There might even be cookies,"* the tall girl repeated snidely. The others cackled cruelly.

As the gang dragged Leila toward Mother Margaret's office, she dug her heels into the linoleum. But together, the girls were too strong. The soles of her shoes left black streaks across the gray tile floor. The tallest girl flung the office door open, and the others yanked Leila through the room toward the familiar closet door. They threw her into the closet and slammed the door shut, drowning Leila's vision in darkness. Leila heard the door lock from the other side.

"Okay, joke's over, let me out!" Leila begged, banging on the door. "Don't you want to see the magicians?"

"Sure we do!" called one of the girls through the thick wood. "That's where *we* are headed right now."

"Come join us...if you can!" called another. Laughter rang out like the cries of crows that often sounded across the playground outside. Their footsteps faded as they ran away.

Leila knew what would happen when she tried the knob, but—always hopeful—she tried it anyway.

It was locked. And she was alone. Again.

Leila swiveled her head back and forth, but the dark was so complete her eyes didn't register any movement. Her heart thundered as it usually did whenever the gang of girls shoved her in here. The acrid smell of the damp wooden walls stung her nose.

In the past, it had taken an adult an hour or more to discover Leila cowering in the corner of the closet. And whenever they *did* find her, they scolded Leila as if she had locked herself in the headmistress's closet.

To calm down, Leila imagined herself as a beautiful girl who was part of the magic show downstairs: purposely shut inside a cabinet on stage, then wowing the audience by disappearing without a trace, with a flash and a bang and a *whizzz-zup!*

Frustration clenched her body. The magic show was the only thing she'd been looking forward to recently. She wanted to see white doves fly from the formal jackets of the magicians, flower bouquets appear from thin air, playing cards float up and out of a deck....

Leila decided she was *not* going to allow those girls to ruin this for her. For the first time, she'd stand up, *really* stand up to them. But before she could do that, she had to figure out a way to escape.

Leila felt around in the dark, pushing her finger against the keyhole. Perhaps there was a way to unlock it from the inside. Leila had never picked a lock before, but she'd read about heroes doing it in stories. First, she'd need some tools. She plucked out the bobby pin holding her hair in place and stuck it in the keyhole. She turned it back and forth. Inside the lock, the tool met the tumblers. She heard them clinking. But without another pin, she wouldn't be able to catch them and turn the locking mechanism.

She didn't have another bobby pin. But she was standing inside Mother Margaret's *office* closet. Sweeping the floor with her fingers, her heart sped up as she encountered a lone paper clip. Luck was on her side!

She unfolded the clip. She stuck the tip into the keyhole and felt around, putting tension on the plug, seeing how far it would give. The pins clicked against the tumblers but kept slipping.

A muffled cheer came from the floor below. The show had begun.

"No, no, no!" Leila whispered to herself. In her mind's eye, she pictured the mob of magicians standing on stage, pulling rabbits out of hats, transforming marbles into pearls, levitating chairs, and flipping black silk cloaks over their shoulders. She'd been counting on some magical memories to get her through the next few months with a smile on her face.

The more she rushed, the harder it was to

manipulate the pin and clip in the keyhole. Minutes ticked by, until it felt as though she might never escape. She worried the show would end before she broke out. Leila was about to throw down her tools in frustration when she felt a distinct *click*, and the door swung open a crack. She tapped her feet excitedly against the floor in a celebratory dance.

At the top of the stairwell, a voice sounded from below: "And now for our final act..." The sound of clapping grew louder as Leila raced halfway down, then paused. In the rec room, several rows of chairs were arranged around a platform, upon which sat a distinctive man in a black suit and a tall top hat. A black cape fell from his shoulders, and when he moved his arms, a red silk lining winked at her. The man's hair was pure white and made of curls, while a straight black mustache smirked from the top of his lips. Leila plopped herself onto a middle step and watched the man with the curly white hair through the rickety wooden balusters.

You must already know who the man with the curly white hair is...but Leila didn't. This was the moment she saw Mr. Vernon for the very first time, and the sight took her breath away. Do you remember when

Carter first encountered Mr. Vernon? It was on the night that Carter arrived in Mineral Wells. He came down from the train yard to blend in with the crowds at Bosso's circus. Mr. Vernon's deft skills—flipping two coins around and around between his knuckles—blew Carter's mind.

Now, as Leila watched this same man's two assistants tie him tightly to a metal chair, she felt something even more profound than Carter had. She was certain that she'd escaped from the closet upstairs so that fate would allow her to see this man.

The stage assistants' faces were covered with a thin black stretchy fabric. First, they cuffed the man's ankles to the chair's legs. Then they wrapped a long chain around his torso and the chair's back, so that his arms were pinned to his sides. The orphans in the audience gasped as the assistants attached a thick padlock to the ends of the chain, which hung in the center of his chest. When they slipped an oil-cloth sack over the man's head, several of the children cried out in fear.

Mother Margaret stood and waved her arms. "Mr. Vernon is a professional!" she said. "Do not be alarmed!"

The man's voice came from under the hood. "*Do* be

alarmed!" he corrected. "For if I haven't freed myself by the end of this very minute, I shall run out of oxygen." Mother Margaret looked sheepish as she sat back down, as if thinking she'd made a mistake inviting this man to possibly perish in front of her wards.

Leila clung to the balusters, peering through like they were the bars of a cage. The two assistants held up a large white sheet before draping it over Mr. Vernon's body. The sheet covered him from head to toe. One of the assistants brought out a large hourglass timer, then set it down on the floor so that everyone could watch as the sand slipped through, second by second by second.

Leila held her breath. The figure under the sheet wriggled and writhed. The clanging of the clasped chains rang through the room. She couldn't help but think of herself trapped in the closet upstairs minutes earlier.

As the final grains poured into the bottom of the hourglass, the children chanted, "*Five! Four! Three! Two! One!*" The figure under the sheet grew still. Seconds passed. The audience stood, a few at a time, jaws agape, wondering if this was all part of the trick.

Leila cried out, "Take off the hood! Someone help him!"

Frantic, the two assistants raced back onto the stage. They raised the sheet, held it up before the seated man, and peered cautiously behind it. Turning to the audience, they shook their masked heads, as if to say, *We're too late!* The orphans went wild, some screaming, as the assistants dropped the sheet to the floor.

The chair where Mr. Vernon had been seated was empty!

The room erupted in gasps of surprise until one of the assistants turned to the audience and removed his mask. As soon as the pure white curls sprang out from beneath, Leila knew that they'd all been had. The magician *did* escape—and in the most unexpected way. The crowd cheered as if someone had just announced that all of them were being adopted that day.

The man with the curly white hair stepped to the edge of the stage, grinned, then took a long bow. Leila was so floored she nearly slid down the stairs. Instead she stood and clapped harder and longer than anyone else.

When the applause ended, Leila pushed her way through the crowd, elbowing the tall girl and her gruff goons aside, to approach the man. "How did you do that, Mr. Vernon?"

His eyes lit up when he saw her face. He paused as if lost in a trance, then answered quietly, "I'll bet you know exactly why I *cannot* tell you."

Leila thought hard. "A magician never reveals his secrets?"

The man chortled. He tapped her forehead lightly. "A bit psychic, are you?"

"Not that I know of," said Leila, rubbing at the spot where he'd touched her. She felt the other orphans pushing in from behind her. She fought to block them out of her mind. "Were you really in danger?"

"Oh, but I am *always* in danger," he said with a wink.

Leila laughed. "I want to learn how to escape like you did."

"I see." He squinted. "Well, it takes years of practice. Is that something you'd be prepared to do?"

"Oh yes! I'd practice *every* minute of *every* day to be like you!"

"Well, enthusiasm is rarely a bad thing," he said, considering. "What is your name, dear?"

"Leila," she answered quietly.

"*Leila*," he echoed. "How pretty! And how long have you lived here with Mother Margaret?"

"All my life."

He was quiet for a moment. "I'd like to come see you again, Leila. Would that be all right?"

Leila's face flushed. "It'd be more than *all right!*" she exclaimed. "Maybe you can teach me a trick or two?"

"Maybe..." He grinned again, the corners of his eyes crinkling with amusement. With both hands, he pinched his fingers together. As he moved his hands apart, Leila noticed that he held a soft white rope between them. He dropped one end and lowered the rope slowly into her outstretched palm. "For you. See what you can do with this. Might I suggest learning different types of knots? They can be helpful in many situations."

Leila's face flushed a deeper pink. She wanted to throw her arms around his neck and say thank you, but she didn't want to make him think she was a weirdo.

At that moment, the other orphans crowded forward, asking for Mr. Vernon's autograph and edging Leila away. She didn't mind. He was going to come back and see her again. He'd teach her a trick. *Maybe.*

She'd be ready. She'd have some new knots to show him in response.

Later, in the bedroom she shared with five other orphans, Leila pulled a tin box out from a hiding place behind a brick in the wall beside her bed. She opened the lid, revealing a few loose, glittering keys.

One key was very special to her. You see, when someone placed Leila on the doorstep of Mother Margaret's Home as an infant, they'd wrapped her in a blanket and left a string looped around her neck, with a key tied to it like a pendant. Of course, Leila didn't remember any of that; she knew the story only because Mother Margaret had shared it with her. It was this first key that'd made Leila start looking for spare ones, or ones that appeared to be lost. She hoped that someday she'd have an interesting collection of all shapes and sizes.

Staring down at her keys, Leila thought about the magic show and how Mr. Vernon had managed to break out of those impossible chains. For the first time, she felt like she'd unlocked something inside herself: a wish to escape. *Really* escape.

When the man with the white curly hair returned later that week with his husband, offering to adopt her, her wish came true—like magic.

TWO

One night, years later, in the apartment over Vernon's Magic Shop, Leila Vernon stretched out atop her big bed, unable to sleep. Thoughts of dark closets kept popping into her head whenever she closed her eyes. A thin patchwork quilt covered Leila's wiry frame, barely protecting her from the brisk air that crept through the open window of her bedroom.

The window looked out over Main Street and the green park that extended far out in both directions. The orange glow of streetlights shifted on the walls and ceiling as the shadows of leafy branches danced to a quiet music composed by the crickets and peeping tree frogs that called out to each other from the nestled hills surrounding the town of Mineral Wells.

Before bedtime, Leila's two fathers had tucked the blanket around Leila's body and kissed her good night, wishing her pleasant dreams. But Leila knew that no wish could protect her from memories of her old life. The dead of night was when they usually came to visit. Sometimes the memories were uninvited guests who stayed long after receiving cues that it was time to go. Sometimes they tried to sneak in, like cloddish cat burglars who had no clue how to finagle a locked door. And sometimes the memories seeped like sulfur smoke through cracks in the walls, threatening to choke and smother Leila, stinging her big brown eyes.

When the other memories became too much to handle, Leila would recall her adoption by the Vernons. She held on to the hand of that memory, as if it could lead her to safety. Sometimes it worked. But sometimes the darkness in those locked closets was too difficult to see through.

Especially after everything that had happened with B. B. Bosso and his circus of thieves several weeks before...

Leila blinked at the ceiling, feeling both blessed and cursed—happy to have this home and this family, but annoyed that the past kept knocking to be let in. *This won't do*, she thought. She whipped away the quilt, then scurried to her bookshelf, where she'd placed her secret tin box.

The box rattled noisily. She drew it to her chest to quiet it. Next door was the room of her newfound cousin, Carter. She didn't want the clamor to wake him.

Leila lifted the lid and stared at her key collection, which had grown substantially in the years since she'd moved to Mineral Wells. But her first key, the one tied to the string, the one that had been with her on the night Mother Margaret found her on the orphanage doorstep, sat on the very top. Leila lifted the string and let the key swing back and forth like a mesmerist's pendulum.

She thought about Bosso and Carter and the other Misfits. She knew that Carter must also suffer from memories of his former life. She wondered if he ever thought of his missing parents, as she sometimes wondered why her own had deserted her on a dark, cold night. Other times, she was happy to not think of them at all. She pressed her hand against the cold key, as if to make an impression against her skin, one that she might use to forge a copy. Her body warmed the key, and the key warmed her body and calmed her mind.

From somewhere beyond her bedroom door, the sound of a commotion stirred: a chair suddenly shifting, a pile of books toppling from a shelf, things crashing to the floor. Next came a sharp and fearful yelp.

THREE

Leila raced into the darkness of the hallway, where she was instantly barraged with small, sharp objects flying at her, pecking her like angry birds. With a yelp, she swung her hand at the nearest light switch. The hall flooded with a soft glow.

Carter was crouched at his own bedroom door, shooting playing cards from his hands toward Leila. (Not angry birds after all, thank goodness!) She swatted them away. "Carter, it's only me!"

He stopped immediately. "Oh geez, I'm sorry!"

His blond hair was a mess, his cheeks red and

marked by rumpled bedsheets. He must have been woken up by the loud sounds as well. Of course, he had come out of his room prepared with his favorite weapon—a deck of cards. He asked, "Are you okay?"

Leila nodded. "You heard the crash and the yelp too?"

Before he could answer, there was another crash. The clamor came from behind Mr. Vernon's office door. It was as if the man were barreling into furniture and knocking things over.

Leila and Carter pounded on the door. From inside, her dad gave a muffled grunt. Carter tried the knob, but it was locked. Leila whipped out her lucky lockpicks from the pocket of her nightgown. With a few swift movements, Leila worked her magic, and the door swung inward.

Dante Vernon was standing in the corner, his curly white hair mussed, his dark eyes as wide as the crystal balls that he sold in the magic shop downstairs. His chest heaved as if he'd just sprinted around the block. "Oh good," he said with a sudden smile. "At least now I know I'm not dreaming. Please shut the door. We can't let *it* get out of the room with my book."

Despite her confusion, Leila did as she was told.

"*It?*" asked Carter. "What do you mean by *it*?"

Mr. Vernon pointed beneath his desk. Something in the shadows let out a horrifying screech.

Both Leila and Carter jumped.

"I'd been writing in my notebook when I dozed off. I woke up when something snatched the book out from under my hand," Vernon explained. "The creature snuck in through the window, which I've closed and locked. It's of vital importance that we get my book back. Understood?"

Leila and Carter nodded.

"Carter, toss me the little rope on the table beside you," Vernon directed. Carter threw the white cord, and Vernon caught it one-handed. "Now, Leila, when I say go, slide the chair away, okay? On the count of three."

Leila nodded even though she wasn't nearly as ready as she would've liked. But that was what it meant to be a Vernon and a member of the Magic Misfits. You trusted your friends and your family...even when they asked you to help catch a mysterious creature that had snuck into their office in the middle of the night.

"One..."

Leila edged toward the chair.

"Two…"

Something growled from under the desk. Leila felt her stomach move up into her throat.

"Three!"

Leila yanked back the chair as Vernon dove under the desk. A blur of blondish fur raced over his spine, back toward the wall, and leapt into the shadows behind a large houseplant.

"What *is* that?" Carter yelped, more curious than frightened. Leila leaned forward. The creature's silhouette was about a foot high and resembled a gremlin.

Mr. Vernon got up, pushing his hair out of his face. He flicked his wrist and the soft rope became rigid in his grip, a loop forming at the end like a lasso. "Children, back away now. I've got this."

"Hold on, Dad." Leila's voice quivered. She picked up the knocked-over lamp and aimed its bulb at the shadows.

Instantly, they could see *it* clearly. The creature looked up at them with fear in its dark eyes—a skinny little thing with a long, slim tail and a black spiked collar around its neck. *It* shrieked again. It was a monkey.

Friends, I'll bet you're thinking that if you were

ever in this situation, you'd plop
yourself onto the floor, hold
open your arms, and coo,
"Give me a hug, you *cuuuuuu-
tie!*" Let me assure you: Night-
time monkey thieves are not
nearly as adorable as you'd
like them to be.

"It's Bosso's monkey," said
Carter, his voice shaking. "I'm
s-sure of it."

Vernon raised his finger to his
lips, trying to not startle the monkey, who snarled
and hitched back as if getting ready to jump at them.
That was when Carter snapped his fingers, revealing a
shortbread cookie in his other hand.

Carter was doing a simple trick called *palming*. Every
good magician has practiced palming at one time or
another. Have you? It's a form of *misdirection* in which
a magician hides an object by cupping it in the palm
of his or her hand. The magician will then reveal the
object by using their other hand to create a distraction.
In this case, Carter snapped his fingers to capture the
monkey's attention, then showed him the cookie.

After being practically homeless for so many years, Carter always seemed to keep a cache of goodies in his pockets, Leila noted to herself. Looked like it came in handy too.

The monkey's snarl faded as he focused instead on the treat in hand. Carter snapped his fingers again, and one cookie became two. The monkey made a cooing sound as he inched close enough to reach out and snatch the cookies from Carter. He shoved both into his mouth, chewed them up, and swallowed. His eyes glassed over with satisfaction.

Leila laughed. The creature wasn't so scary after all. She approached the monkey, sneaking up from the other side as Carter snapped his fingers and revealed another cookie. He let the monkey snatch that one too. He revealed a fourth cookie. The monkey was so mesmerized by the sweet treats that he didn't notice Leila until she grabbed the notebook and tossed it to her father, who tucked it inside the wide pocket of his robe. The monkey swung his head back and forth, conflicted. He looked from the book to Carter's hand, full of cookies. Finally, the monkey caved to his instincts and settled for the cookies. (And who wouldn't? Cookies are delicious.)

Carter dropped one cookie after another across the floor, leaving a path toward Mr. Vernon, who was waiting with the magical, stiffened rope. Her father nodded for Leila to stay where she was, in case she needed to grab the furry little thing. Closer and closer it crept. Vernon was ready to collar the creature when—

A knock came at the door, and a voice called out, "Dante? Everything okay in there?" With a squeak and the sound of scrabbling claws, the monkey retreated into the shadows on the other side of the room.

The office door swung open, and in rushed the Other Mr. Vernon, Leila's poppa. He stood there with a worried look on his face, dressed in a white tank top and black-and-white-checkered pajama bottoms. When he saw the state of the office, his sleepy eyes grew wide.

"Close the door, Poppa!" Leila cried. Before he could, a blur of blond fur raced past his ankles and into the hallway. Poppa let out a scream.

"After it!" shouted Mr. Vernon.

Leila and Carter rushed past her dazed poppa and out into the hallway. They followed the racket that echoed from Leila's room. To her horror, she realized that her bedroom door was open, and so was her window.

The trio reached her doorway just in time to see the monkey's tail slip past the edge of her windowsill out into the night.

✦ ✦ ✦

Leila sat on the comfortable couch in the living room with Carter as Poppa heated milk on the stove in the kitchen. Her poppa, who her friends called *the Other Mr. Vernon*, was the chef at the Grand Oak Resort. He was no magician, but he was a wizard at making late-night snacks. "Almost ready!" he called out.

Her dad, *Mr. Dante Vernon* to most others, stood at the window in the parlor. As he spoke on the telephone, he looked outside at the dark street as if waiting for someone to come along looking for their missing monkey.

"Do you think Bosso is back?" Carter whispered with a shudder.

"I hope not," Leila answered.

"I see. Yes, thank you again for taking my call so late at night," Mr. Vernon said, then hung up the phone and walked into the living room. "As far as the officials can tell me, Bosso is still locked up, far away from here, with the rest of his evil circus crew."

"Except for his gang of frown clowns." Carter shivered. "They got away."

"And his monkey too, apparently," Mr. Vernon added. "As we've just seen, that wily creature is *not* easy to catch."

"Why was he trying to steal your notebook, Dad?" asked Leila.

Mr. Vernon removed the notebook from his pocket. It appeared to be one of the business ledgers from the magic shop downstairs—its cardboard cover had a marbleized pattern. Leila knew her dad kept dozens of them behind the shop's counter.

Vernon flipped the notebook open. Page after page, names and prices of items were listed in simple columns. "Now that, dear daughter, is a mystery. If I could get inside the heads of animals and decipher their thoughts, I'd be one of the most powerful practitioners of magic in this country."

"Maybe he wasn't trying to steal the notebook," said Carter. "If he got left behind by the circus and hasn't eaten in a few days, the monkey probably got lost looking for food. Poor thing is alone and confused and just needs a home."

Mr. Vernon smiled. "Anything is possible if you believe it so. In the meantime, we'll need to sleep with the windows closed."

"But won't it get stuffy in here?" asked Leila.

Mr. Vernon shrugged playfully. "We've all dealt with worse, no?"

The Other Mr. Vernon came through the doorway holding a tray of treats: steaming mugs and a plate of chocolate chip cookies. "Milk and honey for my honeys! Drink up and then everyone back to bed."

As Mr. Vernon slid the parlor window shut, Leila thought she heard a cry in the night. Could it have been the mysterious monkey, angry at them for chasing him? Or had it merely been the old window, squeaking in its frame? At that moment, Leila wasn't sure which she'd rather believe.

Instead, she sipped the creamy and sweet froth from the mug her poppa had handed to her, allowing it to calm the fluttering in her belly.

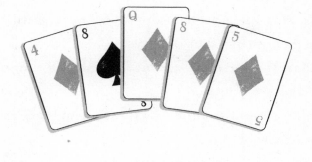

FOUR

"Pick a card, any card!" Carter said, fanning out a deck.

Ridley Larsen raised an eyebrow and tilted her head with a withering stare. "Before we start sharing tricks, we should officially call *Magic Misfits meeting number eleven to order.*"

"If you say so, boss," Carter said with a grin. He split the deck into five small packs, then spiraled them around one another in a single grand gesture before flipping his palms over and revealing empty hands. Sometimes, it seemed to Leila, Carter could have made even the gazebo in the town green vanish with little more than a flick of his wrist.

"Boss?" asked Izzy Golden. "I think of Ridley more as our queen."

"*Queen* is too generic," said Olly Golden. "*Empress* has a nice ring to it."

"Your ears'll *ring* when I give you a sock to 'em," Izzy said, waving her fist in the air playfully at her twin.

"*Rings* and *socks*? But I'm already fully dressed!" Olly noted.

Summer break had started, and Main Street was flooded with shoppers who were down from the resort and kids tasting the freedom of a school-free sunny afternoon. At almost every corner, food vendors handed out samples of their wares: ice cream, chocolates, caramel corn, fruit-flavored ice-slushes.

But the Magic Misfits had no sense of what was happening outdoors. With all six of them crowded into the secret room behind the rear bookcase in Vernon's Magic Shop, they were practically bumping elbows in the dim light. None minded, though; they were practicing what they loved most: magic.

Ridley reached inside Carter's sleeve and removed

the deck of cards he'd hidden there. "Hey! No fair!" Carter cried out. "Stealing is not cool, Ridley."

"Stealing?" Stone-faced, Ridley flipped through the cards and held them out to the group. The playing cards had somehow transformed into a handful of purple note cards—each marked with dots and dashes in black ink. "I brought *these* Morse code study cards from home. *Your* playing cards are right where you left them, Carter."

Crinkling his brow, Carter raised his sleeve to find his deck of playing cards right where she'd said they'd be. Not only was Ridley an expert with transformations, she was also skilled at transforming the color of people's cheeks. In fact, Carter's pale skin had instantly become a fierce pink.

"Nicely done!" said Theo Stein-Meyer.

"Thank you," Ridley said. "Would you mind passing these out?"

Theo guided his bow over the study cards, and one by one, they floated to the members of the Misfits. Theo's levitation ability was one of his most closely guarded secrets. When he finished, he slipped his magic bow back inside the leg of his tuxedo pants.

"I hope everyone has been studying this week," Ridley

went on. "The sooner we learn this Morse code stuff, the better we'll be prepared to communicate secretly."

"Oh, Ridley," said Leila, "I don't think we need to worry about another situation like the one with Bosso."

"And yet only a few nights ago, his pet monkey tried to break into Mr. Vernon's office to steal one of his ledgers." Ridley squinted at them. "Are you sure you're not just inventing excuses to get out of doing your club homework?"

"I thought summer was supposed to be *homework-free*," said Izzy.

"No, no, Izzy," said Olly. "You're thinking of *sugar-free*!" "But we love sugar!" said Izzy. "Mom and Dad hate it, though. Strange, because I always feel *funnier* after I eat sweets."

Leila smiled from the back corner of the far wall. She used to hate small spaces, but now she didn't mind them so much. Blocked by Ridley's wheelchair, she mentally worked out a path through her friends that would allow her to escape the crowded room in less than five seconds. She was always solving puzzles in her head, as if she might one day use them on a stage.

"Leila, would you like to go first?" Ridley asked.

Leila glanced at her note card. The code read:

•• ••—• / —•—— ——— ••— /

•—— ——— •—• —•— /

— ——— ——•• • — •••• • •—•

Leila figured out the translation in her head. "*If you work together...*"

Carter read his secret message. "*And stay true to one another...*"

Theo went next. "*Nothing will bar you.*"

Then Ridley: "*Alone you are weak.*"

Followed by Olly and then Izzy: "*Together...you are...*" They struggled over the final word until Izzy finished, "*Together you are...strange*?"

"Almost," said Ridley, raising an eyebrow. "Together you are *strong*."

"Nice," Carter said to Ridley. "It's the message from the psychic at the carnival. I'm happy you remembered it!"

Just outside their secret headquarters, Mr. Vernon finished ringing up his customers. After they left, Mr. Vernon knocked on the wall and called out, "You do realize it's a beautifully perfect day outside. Some people believe it's a *crime* to be indoors on a day like this!"

Leila perked up. The escape route she'd been scheming suddenly came into sharp focus. She ducked down, shimmied beneath the chair Theo was perched upon, then popped up, leaping over Ridley's wheelchair and rebounding off the wall behind Carter before turning sideways, taking a deep breath, and squeezing between Olly and Izzy. She slid open the secret door and caught Vernon's eye. "And would you consider yourself to be one of those people, Dad?"

"Of course not, my dear." Mr. Vernon winked and then rubbed at his eye as if a speck of dust had suddenly gotten stuck. "I was only commenting on the crime rate in this country. Practically soaring."

"*Practically soaring!*" echoed Presto, the store's prized green parrot. The beautiful bird held court from her perch near the store's entrance. Mr. Vernon cooed at her, holding up his hand for the parrot to nuzzle briefly. He whispered something into her ear, then climbed the spiral stairs to the store's balcony.

"*Waaaaak!*" Presto answered with a curious blink and a nod before going strangely silent.

"Leila, I know your magic-club meeting has begun, but would you and Carter please keep an eye on the store for a moment?" asked Mr. Vernon. "I think my bottle of vanishing ink has actually vanished."

"Of course it did." Leila giggled. "And of course we

will!" She turned to Carter, Theo, Ridley, Olly, and Izzy and then waved them out of the secret room.

"*Boooo*," said Ridley, rolling her chair into the store. "I like it better when our meetings are in there. In the dark. It's more magical."

"More magical than when we are in an *actual* magic shop?" asked Theo. Olly and Izzy grabbed hands and twirled into the space, then pretended to be dizzy and fell down. Leila slid the bookcase door shut as Theo held his magic violin bow over Ridley's head. Her notebook levitated out of her lap and floated just beyond her reach.

"Give that back!" Ridley snarled, grabbing Theo by his tuxedo tail.

"Easy, tiger," Carter said, snatching the notebook from the air and returning it to Ridley. "Play nice."

Ridley thumped Theo's bow tie, changing it from a solid black into a garish mustard plaid. Theo flinched as he glanced at himself in the giant mirror nearby, then adjusted the lapels of his tuxedo jacket. He always looked like he was on his way to a grand party. "I suppose I can make these colors work too," he said to himself, then winked at Ridley. She winked back.

"Since we've gotten our homework out of the way," said Leila, "let's start the actual meeting."

"Hey! That's my line!" Ridley quipped. "Let us bring this meeting of the Magic Misfits to order," she said, elevating her voice to sound like the mayor during a celebratory speech out on the town green.

"Hear, hear!" said Theo.

"You forgot to do roll call," said Carter.

"Fine!" Ridley groaned. "We'll continue with roll call." She read out everyone's names, and they all raised their hands. She spent the next few seconds writing down everything she'd just said in her notebook.

"Let me do that," said Carter.

Ridley reluctantly handed over the notebook and pen. "Who has a club announcement?" she asked.

"Well, we already told you guys about the monkey break-in," said Leila. "That's all my big news."

Ridley barreled onward. "Anything else we should note?" When the group said nothing, she said, "*The Magic Misfits keep no secrets*. Remember?"

"I'm totally secret-free," said Carter.

Leila thought of her tin filled with keys upstairs, the one no one knew about except for her. "Nope," she said. "No secrets here."

"I think some secrets are worth keeping," said Theo,

his voice cool and collected. "I certainly do not intend to give my tricks away within the near future."

Before Ridley could scold her friend, the door to the shop opened, and the little bell rang.

Leila leaned around the end of the aisle and saw a couple standing there. The man and woman looked like a pair of tourists down from the Grand Oak Resort. Since Mr. Vernon was still upstairs, searching for his vanishing ink, Leila raced over and said, "Welcome to Vernon's Magic Shop, where we purvey the impossible. Can I help you find anything?" With a wink, she added, "Or perhaps help you make something disappear?"

Presto rustled her feathers from her perch. "*Shall Houdini confess next, I can find a dozen flying, fake deer!*" she screeched. "*Shall Houdini confess next, I can find a dozen flying, fake deer!*"

"Don't mind our bird." Leila smiled at the customers, who looked indifferent. The parrot's mishmash of words reminded Leila of poetry—well, really *weird* poetry. This wasn't the first time Presto had spouted out such strange things.

Carter appeared next to the customers. "Feel free to look around."

Leila couldn't help but feel happy that Carter was fitting in so quickly. The couple walked with caution toward a table displaying glass eyeballs stuffed in huge jars, vials of green slime, and quartz crystals.

"Why on earth does Presto continue to speak like this?" Theo asked, joining the others at the counter. He craned his long neck back, trying to make eye contact with the parrot, then held up his hand. This usually worked with the doves he kept in his backyard, but Presto had been trained differently.

"Maybe she's practicing for Shakespeare in the Park," Ridley said.

"That'd be neat," said Leila. She patted her shoulder. "Presto! Come!"

Presto only shouted out again: "*Shall Houdini confess next, I can find a dozen flying, fake deer!*"

The shopping couple whispered something to each other, then glared at Presto. They headed to the door with a quiet "Thank you." The bell clanged, and then they were gone. Leila's face burned; she felt disappointed that she hadn't been able to charm them into staying longer.

"That bird is nut-so," said Ridley. "Not like my rabbit. Where is my Top Hat?"

Carter chuckled. "One day, one of us will pull out an actual top hat and say, *Here it is!*"

"Har-har," Ridley scowled. "Not funny, *newbie*. Don't make me kick you out of the club so soon."

"It was only a joke," Theo whispered, slipping the rabbit onto Ridley's lap.

Ridley wasn't having it. "If we're going to make jokes during Magic Misfits meetings, they've got to be much funnier. And Presto has to learn to keep her beak shut." Theo raised a chiding eyebrow. "Oh, come on," Ridley added. "You know I love all of—"

PING! As if from nowhere, a large coin fell out of the air. It bounced twice on the table, rolled on its side in a circle, and fell over.

"Dad, did you do that?" Leila called upstairs, but Mr. Vernon was nowhere to be seen.

Ridley picked up the coin and surveyed it. Theo and the others peered over her shoulders.

"It's letters *A* through *Z*," Olly noted.

"And then back again," Izzy added, "*z* through *a*."

"It's a *cipher*," Ridley whispered.

"A what?" Carter asked.

"A code, a secret way of writing," Ridley answered. "See, if I wrote *CAT* using this cipher, it would become *XZG*. And *DOG* would become *WLT*."

"Awesome," Leila said.

A shadow appeared outside the window of the shop. "More customers," Carter said. Wanting to keep their discovery secret, Ridley dropped the coin into the secret compartment of her wheelchair arm.

The bell chimed as the front door opened again. Leila's heart soared as she imagined that the couple had changed their minds and returned. But a new voice called out instead. "Hello? Is anyone here?"

HOW TO...

Make a Card Change by Shaking It

Who was at the shop door? Well, I'd rather not say. You can skip to the next chapter to find out, or you could stay and learn some magic of your own!

Oh, you decided to stay? It really is wonderful to see you again. I adore working with committed students. Have you been practicing the tricks I showed you in the first book? If so, by the end of *The Second Story*, you might have enough tricks to put on an entire show.

WHAT YOU NEED:

A regular deck of playing cards

HELPFUL HINT (WHERE TO STAND):

For this illusion, you'll want to position yourself close to your audience so that they are looking down at the cards in your hands.

STEPS:

1. Holding the deck in one hand, use your other hand to show your audience a random card. Ask them to tell you what card it is.

2. While they are telling you about the card, slide your pinky finger between the top card and the rest of the deck so there is a small gap.

3. Place the first card faceup onto the deck, aligning it with the raised card. You should now be holding two cards slightly above the rest of the deck.

4. Using the middle finger and thumb of your free hand, grab the corners of the top two cards and move them away from the deck, holding them so that they bend a bit.

(Hint: Both cards should align so that it looks like you're holding only that first top card.)

5. Move your hand back and forth, so the image on the card begins to blur for the audience. Show the audience your card. Have one of them call out what it is. Now, move your hand back and forth.

6. While shaking the cards, use your pointer finger to reach for the far corner of the cards and then pull that corner toward you so the two cards flip.

(Hint: Your middle finger and thumb will be the points where the cards rotate.)

7. Slowly stop shaking
   the cards and reveal
   that the card has
   changed.

8. Take a bow!

FIVE

A woman stood by the counter.

"Sorry!" Leila said breathlessly to the stranger. She spouted her usual spiel: "Welcome to Vernon's Magic Shop, where we *purvey the impossible*! Can I help you find anything?"

"Hello," said the woman. "I sure hope you can." She was medium height with dusky golden skin and wavy dark hair that cascaded like waterfall mist past her shoulders. Deep brown eyes stared into Leila's own.

Leila was captivated. Her fingers trembled. Her mouth went dry. She blinked as if her brain could take a picture. The woman's lashes were long and thick, blackened heavily with mascara. Lips as red as gems were pursed in a tiny blossom below her long nose. She wore a long purple shawl covered in yellow fringe draped over her shoulders, with a gauzy lilac scarf tied around her waist. The image of a crystal ball was embroidered on her large purse. Most spectacular of all were the enormous white stars hanging from her ears. She looked like she belonged there, like a prop in the magic shop's window.

"We have everything a magician might need," Leila said, her voice cracking.

"I'm looking for someone," said the woman, her eyes flicking around the store. "A very old friend of mine. His name is Dante. Dante *Vernon*. His last name's on the door."

"That's because he owns this place," said Carter, stepping forward. "He's my cousin, and he's Leila's—"

"Hold on," Ridley said abruptly, wheeling past Carter and Leila to block the woman's path. "Before we share anything else, maybe you can tell us who *you* are first? We've had some trouble around here lately."

"Trouble?" the woman remarked with wide eyes, clutching her shawl to her chest. "How horrible!"

"My friends here can sometimes be too trusting," said Ridley. "But I'm not. What do you want with Mr. Vernon?"

"Sandra?" Mr. Vernon called out from the balcony. He clutched the railing and peered down at them. "Sandra Santos? Is that you?"

"Dante!" exclaimed the woman named Sandra.

Sandra Santos. Leila was expecting that the woman's name would be one she'd heard before, but it wasn't.

Sandra held up her arms to Vernon as if for a hug.

Since Ridley was still in Sandra's way, she simply stood inside the door, looking like someone witnessing a miracle, as Vernon rushed down the spiral staircase.

"For a moment, I thought I was looking at a ghost," he said. "It's been how long? Decades! What are you doing here?" He squeezed past the speechless assembly of Misfits and, looking baffled, stood before the woman. Finally—almost reluctantly—he hugged her.

Sandra smiled, squeezing him back. "Oh, I was in town and thought I'd say hello."

"*Shall Houdini confess next, I can find a dozen flying, fake deer!*" said Presto again from her perch. All of the Misfits stiffened and groaned.

Vernon smiled at the animal. "Yes. Yes, we know. Aren't you a fantastical bird?" Presto ruffled her feathers and then closed her eyes. *Finally.* Vernon placed his palm on Leila's head. "This is my daughter. Leila."

"Hello," Leila said, shaking Sandra's warm hand.

Sandra squeezed gently. "Nice to meet you."

Then Vernon touched Carter's shoulder and brought him forward. "And this handsome lad is my cousin, Carter Locke."

"Locke?" Sandra asked. "As in...?"

"Lyle's boy," said Vernon. "He's living with us now.

Our family has grown by leaps and bounds." Carter stared at Sandra in wonder. He must've been fascinated that she knew his father, Leila thought. "Here is Theo Stein-Meyer and Ridley Larsen. And the sharply dressed duo in the rear are the Golden twins, Olly and Izzy. Good friends, one and all."

"You knew Carter's dad?" Leila asked.

"Yes, I did," said Sandra. "He was like a brother to me."

"A *brother*?" Vernon asked with a wry grin. "I'd use a different word for how you two were."

Sandra chortled. "Oh, Dante! You haven't changed. Always looking for meaning where there is none!"

"But *meaning* is everywhere!" Vernon insisted, taking her hands. "I've simply trained myself to look for it harder than most."

Leila bolted around the end of the counter and grabbed a picture frame off the wall. Her friends stared at her as if she'd gone crazy. But she didn't care. She held out the frame to Sandra. "This is you," she said, pointing at the girl in the lower right of the sepia photograph. "Isn't it?" The girl was sitting with Dante, Lyle, Bobby, and the other members of the Emerald Ring—her father's childhood magical club—the group that had inspired Leila and her friends to form the Magic Misfits. The girl in the photo was holding a crystal ball. It looked just like the crystal ball embroidered on Sandra's burgundy velvet purse.

Sandra's mouth popped open when she saw the picture. "Oh my goodness! You've kept it all this time, Dante?"

"Of course. I had nothing else to remember you all by. My best friends." Was there a tinge of emotion in his voice? Wistfulness? Somberness? "There's nothing like being part of a club."

"So then, you were also a member of the Emerald Ring?" Theo asked, craning his head forward, seemingly trying to recognize the young girl in the photo inside the older woman standing before them.

"I was indeed." Sandra nodded, handing the photo back to Leila. "I have fond memories of playing in this old building. The fondest of my childhood."

"What was Mr. Vernon like back then?" Ridley asked. "Was he as weird as he is now?"

"*Weird?*" Vernon echoed, shooting Ridley a funny look.

"You *are* pretty weird, Mr. Vernon," she insisted. "But that's what I like about you."

"Back then, Dante was as weird as weird can be," said Sandra. "And secretive. So were we all. And we were proud of it."

Vernon nodded. "That is true, I suppose."

"What can you tell us about Bobby Bosso?" Theo questioned. "He arrived in Mineral Wells recently, and he was not exactly the nicest—"

Vernon cleared his throat and reached out to shut the shop's door. "How about we continue this conversation over some iced tea. We have plenty of shortbread cookies to dispose of."

"That sounds lovely," said Sandra.

"Carter? Theo? Would you mind bringing up the folding table from the basement? Use the service elevator. We'll picnic here in the shop," Mr. Vernon said as he traversed the spiral stairs back up to the balcony and the apartment. "Leila and Ridley, please keep Sandra company." He pointed at the woman and winked. "And Sandra, you stay right there!"

"Oh, Dante," she said, giggling, "unlike some members of our old club, I never learned the art of vanishing."

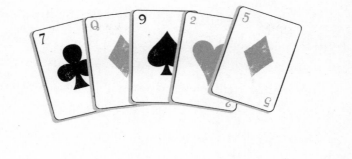

SIX

While Mr. Vernon prepared refreshments in the apartment, Sandra sat with the Magic Misfits at the small folding table in the back of the shop.

"...and then," Leila continued, telling the story of the diamond heist at the Grand Oak Resort, "one of Bosso's goons clobbered my dad over the head! My friends and I knew we had to save him."

Sandra listened in awe to the rest of the tale, as if she couldn't believe that two of her childhood friends would become embroiled in such a bitter clash. Finally, she admitted, "Bobby was always a little...difficult."

"*Difficult* is an interesting way to describe him," said Ridley.

"Totally *bonkers* is another way," Carter answered.

Theo shook his head in disgust. "*Criminal* is the best way."

"He was more *crooked* than corkscrew pasta!" said Olly.

"You mean fusilli," Izzy said.

"*Gesundheit!*" Olly replied. "Speaking of, how does a diamond thief celebrate the Fourth of July?"

"With sparklers!" Izzy answered, with a silly *hyuk-hyuk* laugh.

Mr. Vernon descended the stairs. He was holding a tray with a pitcher of iced tea, several glasses, and a plate of those shortbread cookies Carter loved to hoard. "Gossiping about me again, kids?"

Carter laughed. "Not *you*. We were talking about Bosso!"

"In that case, I'd better step up my game! It's always a trick to be on the tips of everyone's tongues." Mr. Vernon set the tray on the table, adding, "Everyone, help yourselves."

Sandra poured the tea. "Thank you, Dante. You always were the epitome of politeness."

"So, Sandra," Mr. Vernon went on, sitting on the arm of the chair where Leila was perched, "what brings you back to Mineral Wells after all these years?"

"Some sad news, actually," said Sandra, glancing at the kids as if maybe they couldn't handle it. She decided quickly that they could. "My mother passed away."

"I remember hearing that some time ago."

"Yes, it's been several years," Sandra went on. "I had a hard time thinking about returning. Too many...*ghosts* from the past. But Mother left me the old house. You should see the state of it. A total wreck. Boxes everywhere. Layers of dust, inches thick. And quite a few unwanted residents: spiders and flies and mice and snakes. So much work to do. Still, the old house holds a few dear memories—especially those of an old friend who happens to live in the same town. I do apologize for taking so long to visit, but my career has kept me traveling constantly, and I've only recently managed to take the time to settle things here."

"Why do you travel so much?" asked Carter between slurps of iced tea. "Your job, I mean. What do you do?"

"Aha. Well, it just so happens that I'm a stage

psychic. I perform in front of huge audiences all around the country." The Misfits went silent, holding their breath. They stared at Sandra as if she'd just told them that she was the first woman to walk on the moon. "Maybe you've heard of me? I go by the name Madame Esmeralda."

"*The* Madame Esmeralda?" Theo asked. "I thought you looked familiar. Your posters are in some of the theaters where my father conducts his symphony."

"I've never met a famous person before," said Carter.

"Famous?" Sandra laughed. "I suppose I am—though only a *little bit*. It's a fun job. I get to meet lots of people and see the best sights."

"I always thought psychic people were a myth," said Ridley, her brows furrowed. "Are you *really* psychic, or do you just pretend to be?"

"Ridley!" Leila whispered through her teeth. "That's not nice!"

"It's okay, Leila," said Sandra. "It's a question that everyone wonders. At least your friend is honest enough to ask. But yes, I read vibrational energies of people, places, and things, and I perceive information about past, present, or even future events."

"But *how*?" Ridley pressed. "Do you use tarot cards? Numerology? Astrology? Palmistry?" The other Misfits looked at Ridley as if she was spouting nonsense. She scowled, "*What?* When I was researching John Nevil Maskelyne, I spent time looking at some of Mr. Vernon's books about mind-reading here at the shop. There are so many types of psychics: precognitors, who claim to predict the future; telepaths will read your mind; telekinesists move matter with their brains. All quite different. Though most of them are *fraudulent*."

Sandra didn't bat an eye. Instead, she sipped her tea politely.

"How do you identify yourself?" Ridley asked.

"I'm what some would call a *clairvoyant*," said Sandra.

"What's that?" asked Carter.

"It means that I receive little messages about people, and then I let those people know what they need to know."

Leila flinched. "Little messages? From who?"

"Most clairvoyants would say the messages come directly from a *spirit guide*," said Sandra. "The *spirit guide* whispers secrets in our ears, and we share that information with people who need help."

"So you talk to ghosts?" Ridley insisted. "Are the ghostly messages real?"

Sandra pursed her lips mysteriously.

Mr. Vernon grabbed the handkerchief from the breast pocket of his jacket and used it to dab the corners of his mouth. Then he went to shove the kerchief back into the pocket, but another one had already popped up to take its place. Mr. Vernon pulled that one from the pocket too. And another kerchief appeared. He yanked five more kerchiefs from his jacket, dropping them all into his lap with a baffled look. The kids laughed. "The proof is in the pudding," Mr. Vernon said finally.

"What's that mean?" Ridley asked.

"If it looks like pudding and tastes like pudding, it's likely to be pudding?" Mr. Vernon didn't seem sure.

"That is *not* what it means," Theo said. "The adage means you have to try out a new thing for yourself to know whether you like it or not."

"That's not how I understood it," Carter said. "I thought it meant you could only declare something a success after it has been tried out."

"I thought it meant '*Trust me, the pudding is good,*'" Leila said.

"Oh, all pudding is good," said Olly. "Especially chocolate and butterscotch. Yum!"

"But only after Mom removes the gross, leathery skin that forms on top," added Izzy. "Or else Olly won't touch it."

Mr. Vernon laughed. "I guess old sayings are just like magic. It's all in the interpretations. People take what they want from it." He scooped up the extra kerchiefs from his lap and bunched them into one fist. With his other hand, he tugged the edge of one until it flopped loosely between his fingers. Then, with a dramatic flourish, he whipped a single kerchief from his fist and held it up. All the other kerchiefs were gone. The Misfits gasped and then chuckled. "Psychics are like magicians, Ridley. It often doesn't matter whether or not the magician is pretending. What matters is what the *audience* believes."

Ridley turned back to Sandra. "So then, to be psychic, you just have to make people believe that you are?"

Sandra's eyes twinkled. Leila recognized a glimmer of her dad's own mischief. No wonder they'd been close friends once upon a time. "Something like that," Sandra answered. With a wry grin, she added, "How do you know I'm *not* actually psychic, Dante?"

"Are you?" he asked.

She lowered her voice to a spooky cosmic tone and said, *"I've learned much since we were young."* She raised her hands and wiggled her fingers and moaned, like a ghost, *"Ooo-ooo-ooh!"*

The others chuckled. "Where are you staying while in Mineral Wells?" Leila asked. "Not in that old, run-down house?"

"Well, I don't have another option, honey. Not unless Dante is offering." She flashed him a hopeful glance.

Mr. Vernon flushed. "I wish we could, I really do—"

Leila couldn't keep her mouth shut. *"Dad!"* It was unlike him to deny someone help, especially an old friend.

Ignoring her outburst, Mr. Vernon went on. "But we no longer have a guest room, and I couldn't possibly recommend that you bunk on our lumpy couch upstairs. You'd have absolutely no privacy." He shook his head. "Tell you what, Sandra...I'll call my partner up at the Grand Oak Resort and see if he can't arrange for a most extravagant room...just until you've made your mother's place more habitable."

Sandra couldn't hide her disappointment. "I'd be most appreciative."

"Brilliant!" said Mr. Vernon, standing and heading over to the phone. "We'll set you up at the resort. Then, this evening, you'll come back and have dinner with all of us."

"Us too?" asked Theo.

"I'm intrigued to hear more about Sandra's *skills*," said Ridley, raising an eyebrow.

"Alas! I shan't make it," Olly said dramatically.

"Yeah, we can't stay," Izzy whined. "It's a Golden family dinner night."

Ridley pressed the issue. "But the rest of us—"

"Okay, okay." Mr. Vernon chuckled. "Olly and Izzy, you'll be sorely missed. But I'll be sure to ask the Other Mr. Vernon to bring home extra food for everyone else. It'll be a welcome-home party for Sandra."

"I couldn't ask for anything more," Sandra said. "My goodness, how I've missed you, Dante. Thank you so much."

Listening closely, Leila could sense a kind of defeat in Sandra's voice. For a moment, Leila wondered if she had psychic powers of her own.

SEVEN

Across the street from their home, Leila and Carter sat in the grass under the shade of the gazebo. The park was the perfect place for afternoon practice. Leila pulled a loop of string from her pocket and wrapped it around her wrists, trying to figure out a new way to bind herself without anyone else's help.

Carter had brought a pack of cards and was practicing shuffling them, making false cuts and fancy flourishes before returning the cards to their original order. He made the cards spring from one hand to the other. He even tried flipping one card behind his head, though he didn't manage to catch it. When it fell to the grass, his face turned pink with embarrassment.

"Impressive!" said Leila. "You've been practicing."

Carter frowned. "Apparently not hard enough."

"You'll get there," Leila said. After a moment, she added, "Sometimes I wish that I was psychic so I could unlock what's inside my dad's head. I feel like there's so much I don't know about him."

"Like what?" Carter asked. He continued making the cards spring back and forth between his hands.

"Like who he was when he was our age. Has he told you much about his relationship with Lyle, your father? They were best friends after all."

Carter gathered the cards into a single stack. "I wish he'd tell me more. In time, I'm sure he will."

"I want to know about his old magic club. We've already met Bobby Boscowitz. And now Sandra Santos shows up out of the blue. I can't believe we don't even know the names of the other members."

"Have you ever asked him?"

"I only learned about the Emerald Ring when you came to town. I'm not sure he would have confessed very much if we hadn't already figured it out for ourselves."

"Maybe that's what he wants us to do. Find our own answers. Or maybe he's embarrassed about his past. I know I was. Why do you think I kept secrets when I first met you?"

"Hmm, maybe," Leila said, unsure.

"If you were psychic," said Carter, "what would you want to know?"

"I'd want to know that the Magic Misfits won't end up like the Emerald Ring. I'd like to believe that the six of us will never have a *falling-out*." She thought of the girls who'd been so cruel to her at Mother Margaret's Home. She tried not to cringe. "I hope...I hope we'll always be friends."

Carter rubbed his temples. "I predict...that will totally happen!"

Leila smiled. "I'd also want to look into the past. I'd find out why Bobby Boscowitz turned into B. B. Bosso. And I'd learn how come Sandra and my dad weren't in touch all these years. Don't you think it's weird?"

Carter nodded. "Maybe they all just kinda grew apart. Sometimes things happen that we can't control. I mean, *my* dad ended up far away from Mineral Wells. He left the Emerald Ring behind, but I'll bet he never forgot about them. Me? If I were psychic, I'd want to know what happened to my parents."

"Maybe there's a way to figure out all these things without having strange mental powers."

"That would be brilliant." Carter smiled. "I'll help you if you help me."

"Deal!"

"Want to head back inside?" asked Leila. "Poppa will be home from work soon. And I want to clean up before everyone else arrives. Do you think I should wear my straitjacket to dinner?"

Carter laughed. "How will you eat with your arms bound?"

"I'll figure out a way. Maybe I can incorporate it into my act."

As the pair crossed the grass near the gazebo, a loud screech startled them. They froze. It had come from the shadowy space underneath the gazebo. Eyes wide, Carter asked, "Are you thinking what I'm thinking?"

Leila held her breath. "If I am, does it mean I'm psychic?"

Carter blinked. At the same time, they both whispered, "*The monkey*."

Together, they knelt cautiously in the grass and

peered through the diamond-shaped gaps between the wood slats beneath the gazebo. A small shape cowered at the far side. Soft chittering sounds echoed out of the dim space.

"The little thief is back!" Carter said.

"Let's catch him before he tries to steal my dad's ledger again!" Leila unraveled the string from her fingers and quickly improvised a small harness using simple knots that wouldn't harm him. She made loops for his neck and torso and arms.

They treaded softly around the edge of the structure. But as they neared the other side, a blur of fur dashed out and away. The monkey raced across the grass and the street before disappearing behind the barbershop on the far corner.

"Aw, pickles," Leila cried out.

Someone down the street shrieked.

"Crud," said Carter, pulling shortbread crumbs from his pocket. "Next time I'll be better prepared."

"If there is a next time," Leila answered with a sigh. "Should we go after it?"

"Naw. I have a feeling he'll be back."

✦ ✦ ✦

Bursting through the door of the magic shop, Leila called out, "Dad! Dad! You'll never guess who we saw outside!"

Mr. Vernon looked up from a book at the counter and raised an eyebrow. "Well, can I at least try?" Leila and Carter groaned as Vernon held his forefingers to his temples and closed his eyes. "Was it the ghost of Abraham Lincoln?" They shook their heads. "Babe the Blue Ox?" Nope. "Johnny Appleseed?" Uh-uh. "Oh, I know: Oberon, King of the Fairies!"

Carter blurted out, "It was Bosso's monkey!"

Leila nodded. "He was hiding underneath the gazebo and ran off when we tried to catch him."

Mr. Vernon sighed. "We'd better go around and close all the windows. I'll put in a call to animal control. Can't have him disrupting our special dinner tonight."

"Animal control?" Carter echoed. "What will *they* do with him?"

"They'll catch him and lock him up," said Mr. Vernon. "Just like Bosso."

Carter flinched. "Is there such a thing as monkey jail?"

(Dear friends, you'll be happy to know that there is *no* such thing as monkey jail...at least not in Mineral Wells.)

"It might be safer for him to be in a cage than on the street," Vernon pondered out loud.

"A *cage!*" Leila cried. "That's terrible!"

"He just wants a home," Carter whispered.

Leila perked up. "Maybe we could adopt him."

Mr. Vernon chuckled. "Let's take one thing at a time. How about you two clean up the house a bit?

You can even decorate the dining room upstairs for our guest of honor." He grabbed a black top hat off a stand, then tossed it to Leila. "Use pieces from the shop if you want. It's always nice to remember that we're surrounded by magic here."

Leila reached inside the hat and pulled out a never-ending multicolored scarf. Red and green and yellow and blue and purple and orange. Her father was obviously trying to distract them from the idea of the monkey running scared outside. Classic misdirection, Leila thought.

"Hurry now!" Mr. Vernon added, snapping his fingers excitedly. "A good magician should never be caught unprepared when the audience arrives!"

EIGHT

As soon as Theo and Ridley arrived at the shop, Leila put them to work. "We're arranging a Magic Misfits centerpiece for the dinner table." Leila was dressed in her straitjacket, though she'd left the sleeves untied so that she could carry items from the shop.

Ridley looked skeptical. "And why would we want to do that?"

"In honor of two generations of magic clubs." Carter fanned out his hands like a showman.

Leila added, "Plus, seeing how great our magic club

is might get Dad and Sandra talking about the old Emerald Ring."

Glancing around Vernon's Magic Shop made Leila suddenly nostalgic for the time she'd first arrived from Mother Margaret's Home. Walking through that front door, as the little bell sounded over her head, Leila felt like she'd stepped into a wonderland she'd only read about in books. The high-ceilinged room contained every color of the rainbow. The windowpanes were painted bright purple and green. The rugs that covered the rickety wood floor swirled with ochre stripes and red dots and yellow lightning bolts. The glass jars filled with toys and tricks reflected sunlight, casting beams into the far corners of the room, catching the glitter embedded in the plaster walls. For a moment, on that first day, Leila had been certain that it was a dream she'd wake up from; in a way, as time passed, she had.

Friends, you might already understand that it's impossible to live surrounded by such magic without it eventually feeling somewhat normal. Thankfully, her fathers were able to remind her how special she was simply by taking her into their lives and giving her the attention and love she deserved. The magic in the shop was the icing on an already delicious cake.

The quartet gathered supplies from the shop's hidden nooks and secret drawers. Then they took the small service elevator upstairs to the dining room. Leila always giggled when she rode the elevator. How many people had an actual elevator inside their home?

Leila laid the black top hat from the shop on its side in the middle of the long wooden table. The other Misfits surrounded the hat with trick wands, playing cards, knotted ropes, feather flowers, whoopee cushions, tiny cups and foam balls, balloon animals, miniature human skulls made from clear plastic, rainbow-colored glass vials, and a plush green bird that looked like Presto. It appeared as if everything was spilling from the top hat like a magical horn of plenty.

Leila placed her favorite candlesticks—cast iron and shaped like little witch boots—on either end and then lit the tips of the tall white tapers. The light from the setting sun came through the gauzy curtains, and it—along with the glow from the candles—gave the dining room an aura of enchantment.

"Perfecto!" said Leila. "This'll get them talking."

★ ★ ★

When Poppa returned home from the resort, he brought Sandra Santos with him. Her white dress was festooned with giant red polka dots, and she'd pulled her hair up into a tight bun on top of her head. The same white star-shaped earrings dangled from her petite earlobes. According to fashion magazines, every fabulous woman had one or two signature accessories; the stars were Sandra's. She greeted the Misfits with air-kisses. "Oh my!" she said when she saw the table spread. "Fabulous!"

Carter set the needle down on the record player on the sideboard, and playful jazz music danced around the room.

"The Magic Misfits welcome you to dinner!" said Leila with a little bow.

"The best part is how *all of this* will magically return to the shop at the end of the night!" said the Other Mr. Vernon.

Carter winked. "You won't even see it happen."

Leila's poppa brought out plates filled with steaming lobster mac and cheese, fried green tomatoes, Parmesan potatoes, and spaghetti squash with marinara. Everyone gathered at the table, their mouths watering as the Other Mr. Vernon filled crystal glasses with fresh-made lemonade that glowed in the candlelight.

"This all looks so good!" said Sandra.

"The best," said Theo. "As usual."

"Thank you, Mr. Vernons!" Ridley cried out.

"Too bad Olly and Izzy had to miss it," said Leila.

"Yeah," said Ridley, "too bad."

"Dig in while it's hot," Leila's poppa instructed.

The sounds of silverware clacking against plates sounded out like chimes, until Sandra interrupted, "Wait!" and raised her glass. "First, a toast! To old friends!"

Mr. Vernon smiled, his thin black mustache decorating his top lip. "*To old friends*," he echoed. They all clinked glasses, took quick swigs, then got back to the task at hand—filling their bellies with delicious grub.

★ ★ ★

"Oh, how I adored this old building as a child," Sandra mentioned as the Other Mr. Vernon brought out a luscious key lime pie. "Remember the magic shows we put on for passersby? Or our endless games of hide-and-seek?"

"Lyle would always win," Mr. Vernon said with a smile. "He was quite good at vanishing." Leila noticed Carter beam at the thought of his father.

The Other Mr. Vernon cut everyone a piece of the pie and passed them around as Sandra went on, "Best of all, we'd stay up late, telling secrets and making up stories, daring one another to guess which were true and which were lies."

"Let's play!" said Leila, hoping to learn more about her secretive dad.

Sandra glanced at Mr. Vernon as if to silently ask whether it was okay. He shrugged and then nodded. "Only if you go first, Leila," he said.

Leila thought for a moment and then stood. "When I first came to live in Mineral Wells, I was so amazed by my dads and their shop and my new home I was certain I'd wake up from the best dream ever."

"Well, that's obviously *true*," Ridley blurted out. "You've told me that same line almost every week since we met." Leila shrugged and chuckled. "My turn! I once won a soapbox derby contest by decorating my chair as a giant shark."

"That never happened," said Theo. "Or else we would have heard of it already."

Ridley frowned. "It'll happen one day. And you guys will help me put it all together."

"Let us invite Sandra to go next," said Theo.

"Surely!" Sandra cleared her throat. "When I was going through some of my mother's things in our old house, I discovered that she'd kept some drawings I'd done when I was young. I'd copied images from some playing cards that I really loved. I never knew she'd paid close attention to my interests....She was always working, you see....Finding the drawings again..." She paused, as if collecting herself. Leila wanted to reach out and squeeze the woman's hand. "I just miss my mother, I guess."

"That is all true," said Mr. Vernon with a sad smile.

Sandra perked up, shaking off her sudden melancholy as if it were merely a slight coating of pixie dust. "Who's next?"

"I'll go," volunteered the Other Mr. Vernon. "Before it was a magic shop, this building was a jazz club."

"Totally false," Leila said.

"Actually, that's quite true," Mr. Vernon said.

"Dad, how could you not tell me?" Leila asked, flustered.

"I suppose it never came up."

"Now you go, Dad!"

"Me?" asked Mr. Vernon. "Why me?"

"Why not?" asked Carter, throwing a sly look to Leila.

Mr. Vernon tossed his hands in the air, giving up. "Okay, then! Secrets and stories. Truth and lies. Which will it be? Let...us...see..." He leaned forward and stared intensely at each of his guests. "Got one. As you all know, a long time ago, I lived in this very apartment with my parents. Downstairs, my father established a little store that he called Vernon's Magic Shop. You see, my father was the original *Purveyor of the Impossible*. I loved watching him do magic tricks for the customers. I was most impressed when he'd transform one item into another right before their eyes. I begged him to teach me. But he refused, insisting that the best way to learn a trick was by figuring it out for myself."

Mr. Vernon picked up the green bird plush that looked like Presto from the centerpiece and held it in his palm. "And so I did. One day, I decided to show my father what I had taught myself. I took his coffee mug, still holding some coffee, and placed it on a clean plate. Then I dropped a top hat on top of it, like so..." Mr. Vernon placed the stuffed animal on the table, and placed the centerpiece top hat over it.

"My father waited patiently as I waved my hand around the hat, like this, and said, '*Abracadabra!*' Then I lifted the hat from the counter. And the coffee mug was no longer there—instead, a snow globe with a wintry scene of Mineral Wells sat in its place. My father was so proud. I remember clearly how he beamed at my self-earned ability. Little did he know, I broke his mug during the trick, which is why he never saw the mug again. But, I've gotten quite a bit better since then..."

Mr. Vernon whipped the hat off the plate and the entire table yelped.

Instead of the plush bird, Presto the very real parrot sat there and squawked at them. She bounced up and down, as if impressed with herself. Mr. Vernon set the hat back into the center of the table and held his finger out to the bird. The parrot stepped on, and he brought her up to his shoulder. After a fluttering of wings, she perched there.

"Now tell me, kids," said Mr. Vernon, "was that story the truth? Or am I lying?"

Carter knocked on the table, using Morse code to answer:

— •—• ••— — ••••

Ridley burst into applause. "Very good, Carter!"

"It was the truth, Dad!" Leila beamed. "The absolute truth!"

Mr. Vernon bowed his head, and the whole group broke into a round of applause. Leila felt giddy. Having Sandra here was actually working; her dad had opened up about his past. Hopefully, this was only the beginning.

"How did you do that, Mr. Vernon?" asked Theo. "Presto was in her cage downstairs when we came in."

"I know how he did it!" Carter said. "First you need a mechanism—"

"*Indocilis privata loqui*," Mr. Vernon interrupted, holding a finger to his lips.

"What's that supposed to mean?" asked Leila. "Are you trying to tell us some sort of new code?"

Her dad motioned like he was zipping his lips, and

then, with an invisible key, he pretended to lock them up tight.

The Other Mr. Vernon shook his head. "What have I told you about no animals or speaking Latin at the dinner table, Dante?"

"Latin?" Leila echoed. "Since when do you know *Latin*?"

But Mr. Vernon pretended he no longer heard her. "Can't we make an exception?" he asked the Other Mr. Vernon. "My old friend is here to visit."

Sandra snickered. "You haven't changed one bit, Dante."

"You keep saying that. But haven't you noticed this?" Mr. Vernon ran his fingers through his thick and curly hair. "Completely white now."

"Oh, stop," said the Other Mr. Vernon. "We're still young."

"No. *We're* still young," Carter said with a playful smile. "Young and full of vinegar!" Theo and Ridley giggled.

"It's all a state of mind." Sandra nodded. "Mm-mm, this pie! It makes me feel like I'm back in Florida in my old shop on the beach. People used to wander in for readings. They'd stay for hours, chatting with me and drinking tea. That was one of my favorite times. Sometimes I wish life could still be as simple as that."

"It can be if you want it," said Mr. Vernon.

"Do you still do readings?" asked Theo.

"All the time! Would you like me to do some for you?" The kids clamored their approval. "I'm not sure if I'll compare to Dante's little story, but I'll try." Sandra clicked her tongue against the roof of her mouth and squinted. The room went silent as Sandra sat with her eyes closed for about ten seconds. Then she whispered, *"Running, running, running...The smell of smoke, the rush of a train...There are many trains....More than I can count...Counting...The shell game...A feeling of shame...followed by...escape!"* She straightened up and then said in a normal voice, "Does that mean anything to you, Carter?"

Carter's eyes went wide. He glanced around the table at his friends. Their mouths were open, all of them dumbstruck. "Yeah, it does. Before I came to live with the Vernons, I...I traveled by train. A lot. And my uncle used to scam folks out of their cash with that horrible shell game."

Sandra thought for a moment, then nodded. "That time is over for you. Forever."

Carter's eyes grew even wider as relief washed over him. "Good to know," he said, smiling.

"What about me?" Ridley said.

Sandra rubbed her temples as she turned toward Ridley. Immediately, Sandra sneezed into her napkin. "*Stuffy noses and watery eyes*," she whispered. "Does that mean anything to you?"

Ridley shrugged. "My parents have allergies. It's why I have to keep my pet rabbit here at the magic shop." She looked at Mr. Vernon and smiled. "Thanks again for letting me."

"Anytime," he answered.

Sandra said, "You will never suffer from them in the same way your parents do."

"Thank goodness!" Ridley threw her hands into the air. "One less thing to worry about!" Leila could tell her friend was joking, but Sandra smiled, as if Ridley's response was a success.

Next, Sandra's eyes fell upon Theo. "*I hear many voices*," she whispered. "*A house filled to the brim with voices...*"

Theo looked confused. "My brothers and sisters are all coming home to visit this summer. In just a few weeks. My mom and dad are really looking forward to it."

"They are...but *you're* not," said Sandra, pointing at him.

Theo flushed. "Well, I *am*, but sometimes when they're all together, I feel a little bit..."

"Lost," Sandra said. Theo nodded.

"*Music*," she added. "I hear music too."

"I also play the violin," Theo confirmed.

"That will help you through any hard times that come your way. Stick with it."

"Oh, I will. My father is *making* me." Theo grinned as everyone laughed.

When Sandra finally looked at Leila, Leila felt dizzy. But Sandra squinted, and Leila made herself smile wider than usual. She wanted to hear only good things. *"Footsteps. A knocking at a door. There is no answer."* Thank goodness, Leila thought. That didn't mean *anything* to her. The room was unbearably quiet. *"A gift,"* Sandra added, almost as an afterthought. *"A key..."* Leila's heart jumped into her throat. "Does this make sense?"

Leila thought of the key on the string in the tin box, the one that she'd had since she was a baby. But she didn't want anyone to know about it. The secret made her feel strong. Still, she found that she couldn't lie to this woman. "I...I think so."

Mr. Vernon gave Leila a quizzical look, but he didn't pry.

"This *key* will become important in the coming days," said Sandra. "Keep it close."

Leila felt like she'd been struck by lightning. Hating the sudden attention, she changed the subject. "Did you know that we can do tricks too? Theo, Ridley, Carter, and me?"

"That's what Mr. Vernon tells me," Sandra said.

Leila's voice rose. "Carter, show Sandra what you can do."

Carter picked up a spoon from the table. With a flick of his hand, the spoon disappeared. With his other hand, he reached beneath his plate and retrieved the spoon.

Sandra gasped. "That's quite good."

"Now, Theo," said Leila. "Go on."

Theo removed his magical violin bow from the pocket of his tuxedo pants and held it over the centerpiece. Slowly, the top hat flipped upright and began to dance in a small circle around the table.

"Amazing!" said Sandra. "Bravo!"

Ridley shook her head. "I'm not a circus monkey, and I do not perform on cue!" For a moment, everyone thought she was really upset. But when she picked up her napkin and tossed it onto the table, it turned from white to bright blue instantly. "What trickery is this?" Ridley said with a wink. She picked up the napkin again and gave it a shake, and it turned green. "Stop it!" she yelled at the napkin, and it turned red. Everyone laughed.

"And don't forget Leila," said Carter. "She can escape from anything. Look, she's already wearing her straitjacket."

"I'll just need to get my locks from my bedroom. Dad, can you help set me up?"

"Escaping at the dinner table?" asked Mr. Vernon. "I'm not so sure about that."

"*Daa-aad*," Leila said, rolling her eyes.

"That is a *very good* argument," Mr. Vernon said, snapping his fingers. "You talked me into it. Let's go!"

Sandra stood up from the table. "While you do that, would someone point me toward your powder room?"

"It's in the same place it's always been," said Mr. Vernon, nodding toward the hallway. "We haven't done any remodeling since I inherited the building."

"End of the hallway? I'd forgotten. It's been such a long time." Sandra thanked him and made her way down the dark passage.

NINE

Leila retrieved the locks—as well as her lucky lock-picking tools—from her bedroom and then brought them back to the dining room. As Mr. Vernon clasped the final lock onto the straitjacket, there arose a frightening clamor from the shop below. *Crash! Smash! Creaaaaaak...BAM!*

The muffled sound of a shriek rose up through the floorboards. Mr. Vernon's eyes went wide, and he raced down the hallway. Leila followed, trying extra hard not to trip since her arms were bound.

The bathroom at the end of the hall was empty. Sandra wasn't there.

The group rushed to the balcony and peered over the railing to see Sandra sitting on the bottom step, smoothing out her dress and rubbing her shin. Books and papers were scattered on the floor nearby. Sandra noticed everyone watching her and cried out, surprised, "Oh, I'm so embarrassed!"

"What happened? Are you all right?" Carter asked, racing down the spiral stairs to help Sandra up. The others followed him into the shop, while Ridley rolled her chair close to the balcony to get a better view. Leila treaded carefully as she worked the locks off her jacket. By the time she reached the lower level, she'd managed to free herself completely.

"I'm so sorry," Sandra said, straightening her dress and glancing at Vernon. "The bathroom upstairs was out of tissue, so I came downstairs to use the one in the shop. But then I heard something scratching at the front window. I approached and..." Sandra's color drained from her face. "A *monkey* jumped out of the bushes and slapped at the glass! It scared me so badly I ran and tripped, knocking over all these books." She glanced down at the books by her feet. "Can you believe it? I didn't think Mineral Wells even had *monkeys*—let alone one that would try to *attack* me!"

Carter rushed to the front door, unlocked it, and peeked out into the evening. He peered up and down the street.

"We saw him this afternoon," Leila noted. "Funny, though, he didn't seem like he'd try to attack anyone. He was more scared of us than we were of him."

Sandra shook her head. "What a mess I've made!"

"Please don't apologize, Sandra," said the Other Mr. Vernon.

Mr. Vernon took her hand. "Let me see your leg. Are you bleeding?"

Sandra sniffed and shook her head. "Merely bruised. I think I've already gotten all the scars this life has planned for me. No matter. After that fright, I feel like I should head back to the resort. Let me fetch my shawl from upstairs."

"I will get it for you," said Theo.

"I'm already on it," called Ridley from the balcony, turning her chair around and heading back into the apartment.

"Thank you, dears. You're all too kind."

After many generous hugs and handshakes, the

Misfits said good-bye to Sandra. Then Mr. Vernon walked her to her car. The Magic Misfits stood in the shop with the Other Mr. Vernon, watching through the large front window.

"What a night!" said the Other Mr. Vernon when his husband returned.

"She always was clumsy," said Mr. Vernon, crossing his arms as Sandra disappeared into the night. "Strange, though..."

"What's strange, Dad?" Leila asked, slipping out of her straitjacket.

"I'm certain the apartment was ready for guests. That bathroom should have been in order."

"Sandra wouldn't lie..." Leila scoffed. But she thought of Sandra's predictions during dinner and wondered if the woman had made it all up. She looked at her friends. "...would she?"

Mr. Vernon was quiet for another moment, then turned toward the group, color returning to his cheeks. "What reason would she possibly have to do such a thing?"

Leila didn't know. She did understand, however, that once again her dad had magically evaded her question. He was doing that a lot lately. The world of adults seemed to her like a great big puzzle box that locked up tight without a key.

✦ ✦ ✦

After her friends had left, while Leila brushed her teeth in the upstairs bathroom, she noticed that the roll of toilet tissue was empty. Sandra hadn't lied after all. But, she wondered, did this mean that her father had made a mistake? Dante Vernon was many things, but forgetful wasn't one of them.

Leila closed the door to her bedroom and turned out the light. Removing the tin from the shelf, she thought about what Sandra had told her during dinner. *"This key will become important in the coming days. Keep it close."*

She lifted the lid and clutched the string attached to the oldest key in her collection. For the first time in a long time, she slipped the string over her head and allowed the key to drop just inside the neck of her nightgown.

HOW TO...

How to Make a Coin Vanish Under a Glass

While Leila and Carter get some shut-eye, you and I have time for another magical lesson. This one requires some forethought, and of course, lots of practice. (And maybe a little construction...which Ridley loves.) I only request that you do *not* stay up all night preparing. Warning: Sleepy magicians make mistakes! But one learns from mistakes. So even if you don't get it on the first try—don't stress—try, try again!

WHAT YOU'LL NEED:

A coin. (The bigger in size, the better the audience will see it.)

A transparent (that means CLEAR) drinking glass. (You'll probably want to avoid the fancy glasses that once belonged to your long-lost great-granny. I'd suggest using one that your family will not miss very much.)

A dark handkerchief or small towel

Two blank pieces of clean and totally white paper

A pencil

Washable glue

A pair of scissors. (I'm sure you're keen enough to know that a grown-up should be present while using sharp objects. During magic shows, magicians can make it look easy to reattach a severed thumb. In real life, a surgeon is usually involved. Not fun!)

TO PREPARE:

Use the pencil to trace the mouth of the glass onto one piece of white paper. Very carefully, cut the paper along the pencil line. Erase any marks left by the pencil on the cutout. Place a very light coating of glue around the edge of the glass, then attach the paper. Let the glue dry for several minutes.

STEPS:

1. Before your audience arrives, place the other piece of white paper on a flat table. Rest the glass, facedown, on one half of the paper and the coin on the other half.

2. Tell your audience that you shall make the coin magically disappear!

3. Drape the handkerchief over the glass, the coin, and the paper as you lift the glass and place it on top of the coin.

HELPFUL HINT:

As you move the glass, make a little noise with your mouth. *Zip!* Or *Shoop!* Or *Vleep!* Any sound that will surprise your audience member and possibly make them flinch. Personally, I like to shout, "OUCH! It bit me! Just kidding!" This allows you to cover the coin while bringing the audience's attention to your face instead. A little *misdirection* among friends never hurt anyone, has it?

4. Remove the handkerchief to reveal that the coin has disappeared inside the glass.

SECRET MAGIC MOVE:

Since the paper cutout you glued to the glass is the same color as the paper underneath, it hides the coin, making it seem like the coin has vanished.

5. To make the coin reappear, cover the glass with the handkerchief again, then shift it back to its original position. Remove the handkerchief to reveal that the coin has returned!

6. Offer to show the coin to your audience, so they can check for themselves that it is real.

7. Take a bow!

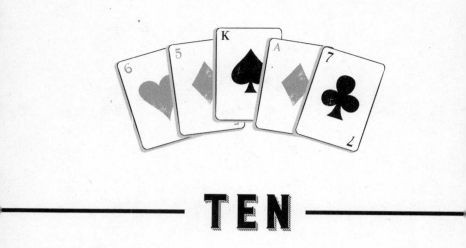

TEN

A few days after the Vernons' dinner party, Leila, Carter, Theo, and Ridley made their way up the hill from town toward the Grand Oak Resort. The sun was beginning to dip toward the western horizon, and the shadows of trees were stretching long across the grass. The sky was painted a deep, comforting blue, and wisps of high clouds were like strokes of white left by feather flowers.

The enormous white lodge was just ahead. The group went around the side and to the back, where they usually met their friends. They trailed along one of the footpaths that connected all the outer buildings to many of the resort's recreational activities. Quaint gables rose up from the dark rooftops, and green shutters accented every window.

Leila thought of these grounds as her second home. The apartment over the magic shop was lovely, but the Grand Oak had everything from pools to a magnificent view overlooking Mineral Wells. Leila often accompanied her poppa when he came to work, if for no other reason than to stroll among the gardens.

On the other side of a shaded floral bower, the Golden twins were cartwheeling through the grass. Izzy planted her feet and crouched down as Olly leapt onto her shoulders. Izzy rose up, swift as a piston, grasping her brother's legs. They stood in the field, watching as the Misfits approached in awe of their gymnastic skills.

Izzy called to Olly, "You've gained some weight!"

Olly patted his belly. "Thanks to all my friends called doughnuts!"

Suddenly, Izzy looked like she could no longer hold her brother up. As they tipped, Izzy dropped to her knees and Olly tumbled into a perfect somersault, landing in a perfect pose, arms outstretched, hands waving. It was all part of the show with these two. Leila and the others broke into enthusiastic applause.

Upon seeing their friends, the twins then burst into an a cappella song, harmonizing in comic falsetto, box-stepping and pirouetting.

> *"Welcome, welcome, one and all,*
> *Nice to see you, guys and dolls!*
> *A lot's gone on; have things been funky?*
> *We heard you almost caught a monkey!*
> *We've missed you much, what a strange week!*
> *Check our pockets; have a peek!"*

Synchronized, the twins held open their vest pockets. Before anyone could get too close, two pink noses stuck up out of the shadows.

Ridley shrieked and rolled back her chair. Theo wrinkled his nose. "Are those *mice*?"

"We wanted magical assistants," said Olly.

"We've spent all day training them," Izzy chimed in.

"To do what?" asked Carter.

Olly and Izzy glanced at each other. "So far, they're very good at squeaking," Izzy said brightly, spinning the statement to sound impressive.

"Where did you get them?" asked Leila.

"We caught them out here in the yard," said Olly.

Izzy nodded. "They practically jumped into our hands."

"I'm not sure why you'd need magical assistants," said Ridley. "Since you're not *officially* magicians."

"Aren't we?" asked Olly. "Laughter is the best magic of all."

"Actually, actual *magic* is the best magic of all," said Izzy.

"Whatever," Olly said. "Besides, I don't need to be saddled with a label. It's good to leave your options open, to try a little bit of everything. Tap-dancing. Singing. Miming. Acting. Library-ing—"

Izzy rolled her eyes. "That's *not* a word."

"*You're* not a word," Olly retorted. "My point is, there are endless possibilities to what we can teach these mice."

"Endless!" Izzy added, "Math! Chemistry! French cuisine!"

"Oh yes," said Olly. "I love a good *boeuf bourguignon*. Hey, Izzy!"

"Yes, Olly?"

"What do you call a mouse who excels at oration?"

"I don't know, Olly. What?"

"A public *squeaker*!"

"Hey, Olly!"

"Yes, Izzy?"

"Where do mice shop for groceries?"

"I dunno, Izzy. Where?"

"The *mini*-mart!"

Leila, Carter, and Theo chuckled politely, while Ridley let out a groan. "I think that your material needs some work. Anyway, I'm very happy you've made some new friends, but I'm here to call our meeting to order if everyone is ready."

Ridley handed her notebook to Carter, who had become the club's unofficial secretary. "Roll call!" Ridley sang out. When she spoke each member's name, that person answered, *"Here!"*

Except for Olly, who said, "Present! Ooh, I love presents. Does anyone have a gift for me?"

"Announcements," Ridley said. "Let's hear 'em!"

Izzy raised her hand. "How did the dinner with Sandra Santos go?"

"You two should've seen it!" said Carter. "She read our fortunes and talked to her 'spirit guides' and tripped downstairs when she saw Bosso's monkey looking in the shop window at her!"

"So that monkey is still around?" Olly asked.

"Apparently," said Leila.

"Sandra sounds like a hoot," said Izzy.

"No, Izzy," said Olly. "A hoot sounds like this: *Hoo-oo! Hoo-oo!*"

"Wow, Olly, you're pretty good at that," Izzy said sarcastically. "Maybe you can befriend an owl and get *wise.*"

"*Har-har,*" Olly said. "Sorry we couldn't be there. Sandra sounds like she knows her way around a good performance."

"She really does," Leila noted. "Have you seen her around the resort at all?"

"She attended our show this morning," Olly said. "She clapped really hard. Very nice of her."

"She even *looks* like she might be psychic," said Izzy. "She's certainly got the right hair for it. Long, wavy, and"—she whispered this next part—"*filled with secrets!*"

"There's no such thing as psychic," Ridley moaned.

"Then how did she know so much about us?" asked Leila.

"A dozen different ways, probably! I mean, she had plenty of time here at the resort to ask around about us before returning for dinner," Ridley suggested. "After everything that happened with Bosso, people know a little bit about us now."

Carter cringed. "Hopefully not *too many* people."

"I did a little more reading last night about some of the self-proclaimed psychics of the past century," said Ridley. "Did you know that Harry Houdini was not only famous for escaping impossible traps but also for debunking fake psychics?"

"He was?" Leila asked. "I've never heard that before, and I *love* that guy."

"We are aware," Theo noted.

"Houdini was part of this club whose mission was to stop people from believing in fortune-tellers," Ridley continued. "In most of the old photos where the spiritualists were supposedly spitting out this ghostly slime called *ectoplasm*, Houdini figured out it was actually made of wet cheesecloth."

Theo chimed in, "I have seen a photograph in a book of a man who was levitating several feet off the ground. But if you examine the image closely, it is apparent that he jumped off his chair in the middle of the shot. Disappointing."

"But what Sandra did seemed so real," said Leila, feeling the key hanging around her neck.

"If you really think about Sandra's so-called readings," Ridley went on, "mostly she just said something vague. Then *we* filled in the blanks for her. We wanted to believe it was true. I don't believe in her mumbo jumbo about speaking to *spirit guides* or *ghosts* or whatever...."

"Oh hey! We do have an announcement," Izzy said, elbowing her brother.

"About having tuna on rye for lunch?" Olly asked. "That's hardly news."

"No, knucklehead," Izzy said. "The ghosts!"

"Oh yeah! The ghosts!" Olly said.

"What ghosts?" Ridley snorted.

Olly jumped up and down, excited. "Word has spread all week that the Grand Oak Resort is being haunted."

"Haunted?" Carter asked. "By who?"

"Or should we ask *by what*?" corrected Theo.

"Come closer, and we'll tell you the tale," Izzy cooed, making her voice low and dramatic. "Our friends on the maintenance staff have seen and heard things in the old abandoned wing of the main lodge—*strange* things."

"'Tis true," said Olly, mimicking his sister's tone. "*Things* that they cannot explain! In recent weeks, staff has heard voices and seen shadows moving about within the building. Only problem is—the abandoned wing has been locked up tight for years."

Theo and Leila both shivered from a sudden chill.

"Yeah, right," Ridley said. "That's hardly evidence of ghosts."

A nearby door banged open and the kids all jumped. "Whew. No ghost," Izzy said. "Just Dean, the bellhop."

A thin old man wearing a droopy green hotel uniform was dragging an old mop behind him. "Dean!" Olly called.

The old bellhop looked at the Misfits as Izzy waved him over. "You've heard the rumors about the ghosts of the Grand Oak Resort, right?"

"Oh yeah!" said Dean. "It's got everyone pretty spooked. Some of the maids are superstitious and too scared to go near the old wing. Mr. Arnold, the manager, is at his wit's end. He's already threatened to fire some of them if they don't do their jobs."

"And just who *are* these supposed ghosts?" asked Ridley, still doubtful.

"Can't say, 'cause I don't know. What I *do* know is that a bunch of bad stuff happened in that old wing. That's why it's still closed to this day." Dean looked over his shoulder as if to see whether anyone was watching him. "Long time ago, there was a *fire* in the rear wing. Lots of damage.

Think someone got hurt. Cops never found out who did it, but rumor is that crazy guy who runs the magic shop in town started it with some of his friends back when they were kids."

"What?!" Leila gasped. "That *crazy guy* is my dad!"

Dean's face flushed as red as the roses in the garden across the lawn. "Pardon me, miss. Didn't mean no offense."

Carter glanced at the group. "Wait a second. *Mr. Vernon* started the fire?"

"It's all just talk," Dean said, unsure. "The hotel rebuilt the wing, but soon after that, there were horrible rains, and the roof didn't hold up. Water damage. They did repairs, but after that was an attack of black mold. Followed by termites, mice, spiders, you name it. Like the place was *cursed*. Finally, the owners decided to just wall off the whole thing and use it as storage. One day, I hear, they'll try to open the wing again, but I doubt it'll happen anytime soon. After all this time, there's pro'ly *all kinds* of ghosts in there." His face dropped, as if he suddenly realized that he was talking with a bunch of kids, and he added, "But if anyone asks you—you didn't hear any of that from me!"

"Later, Dean," said Olly, waving as the bellhop

walked away slowly, dragging his mop with him. "The old guy sure does like to gossip."

"Do you really think my dad had something to do with the fire?" Leila asked.

"No way," Carter said. "Sounds like a hoax to me."

"But what about the ghosts?" Theo asked. "Perhaps the Magic Misfits should look into it."

Ridley threw her hands in the air. "Ghosts aren't real!"

"Remember what Mr. Vernon said," Carter noted. "It's not whether magic is real or not. It's what you believe. Same applies to ghosts."

"Fine, in that case, the Misfits absolutely *should* investigate," said Ridley with a look of intrigue.

"What if we do find ghosts?" Izzy asked. "That'll make the Grand Oak even more famous. Hey! What do they serve for breakfast at a haunted hotel?"

Olly guessed, "Ghost toast!"

Izzy nodded, adding, "With boo-berry jam!"

"I hope the hotel *is* haunted," said Olly.

"It would bring in even more guests to see us perform," Izzy added.

"Not if the staff is fired for being superstitious," Carter said. "I don't like the idea of anyone getting fired for being afraid. We should look into it and get to the bottom of this nonsense."

Ridley saw that Leila was looking at the ground. "Hey, buck up, Leila. I'm sure that old Dean doesn't know what he's talking about."

"I don't know. My dad always seems to have so many secrets...." Leila whispered.

"So let's look into the ghosts. And maybe we'll learn more about the fire."

"Great idea," Leila said, finally smiling again. "It would be horrible if anyone at the Grand Oak had to lose their job because they're too scared to work here." Leila clapped as a brilliant idea burst forth. "We should ask Sandra to *talk* to the ghosts. She can ask them to leave. If there's one thing people in Mineral Wells love, it's a show."

"And pizza," said Olly. "People in Mineral Wells are crazy about pizza."

"And ice cream," said Izzy. "People in Mineral Wells just ado-*oore*—"

"A show," Ridley interrupted. "Good idea, Leila. What room did Sandra say she was staying in?"

ELEVEN

"Sandra Santos speaking," said the voice through the receiver.

"Hi, Sandra! It's Leila calling from the lobby down-stairs."

"Leila! What a surprise! I was just thinking about you. Would you like to come up for some tea? I could read your leaves!"

"That's the thing," Leila answered. "My friends and I were wondering if you wouldn't mind coming down instead. There's something going on in the rear wing that we need your help with."

By the time Leila went outside again, a small crowd of employees and guests had gathered on the back patio. Everyone was whispering to one another, intrigued. Leila leaned into Carter's ear and said, "Where'd all these people come from?"

Carter shrugged. "While you were on the phone with Sandra, Dean the bellhop was telling the other employees that there was going to be a séance and word spread quickly. I guess he was eavesdropping on us."

"Children!" Sandra called from across the patio, holding her arms out as if she might scoop them all up into an enormous hug. Today, Sandra was dressed in a floor-length chartreuse paisley caftan. A green teardrop-shaped gem dangled in the center of her forehead from a gold-colored headband that pinched her hair into a funny mushroom. "Thank you for calling me! You know, I always believed this old place was haunted."

Sandra indicated the rear wing of the lodge. "The séance is going to be so enlightening. And fun!"

"Talking to ghosts is *fun*?" Ridley asked.

"*Helping people* is fun," said Sandra, looking at the crowd, which was continuing to grow. They were all staring at the glamorous-looking woman in the paisley caftan. It turned out that Olly was right: Dean the

bellhop *was* quite the gossip. Sandra pretended to not notice the crowd. "I think we can all agree that's a good thing, no?"

Ridley actually blushed and then nodded.

Leila couldn't hold her tongue any longer. She grabbed Sandra by the hand and led her to the side. "Sandra, can you tell us about the fire? I heard a rumor that my dad started it with his friends. Was it the Emerald Ring?"

Sandra grimaced and shook her head. "I know nothing about that. But if there was a fire, I highly doubt Dante would have had anything to do with it. Now, we have a crowd waiting. Let's get started, shall we?"

Leila's throat swelled with embarrassment; she shouldn't have mentioned it. Not here, not now.

Sandra looked up at the building's facade. Curtains were drawn across most of the windows, and a blackness stared down at them from the windows that were open. Despite the humidity of the afternoon, Leila felt a brisk chill sweep across her skin. Sandra squinted, as if to show that she wasn't afraid, which made Leila feel somewhat better.

Sandra grappled with the knob of the back door, but it appeared to be locked. "Does anyone have the key?"

Key? Leila thought. The pendant under her shirt felt cool against her sternum. Could this be the moment that Sandra had predicted? Was Leila wearing the tool that would somehow open the lodge's back door? But she didn't need a key to do that, she thought—the lucky lock-picks in her pocket would do the job just as easily. Leila wouldn't dare work on this lock in front of a crowd, though. People might start to think she was a burglar.

"Here!" Dean stepped forward, holding up his hand. He rattled a large key ring before opening the door and stepping aside. A dank aroma wafted out. It made Leila think of the closets at Mother Margaret's Home.

Sandra approached the entry. Clasping the two sides of the door frame, she stiffened her spine, as if something inside was affecting her in a profound way. "Oh yes, there are definitely spirits here. I hear them calling out. Do you?" she asked the gathering people. A general murmur rose up. Leila couldn't tell if they were agreeing or disagreeing. Personally, Leila didn't hear any sounds other than the wind through the trees and a train horn calling out in the distance. Turning to the Misfits, Sandra added, "Come. I need the assistance of my new friends. Our connection will only help build up the energy needed to connect with *the beyond*."

Leila glanced at the others. Ridley wore a skeptical grimace. Carter looked curious. Theo looked puzzled, as if he needed to see and hear more before making up his mind. Olly and Izzy both tittered with excitement.

Leila felt a mix of all their emotions. Together, the group stepped toward the door. Sandra had them stand in a circle and clasp hands. She told them, "I need you to concentrate. Listen and be still." She closed her eyes and began to speak. "Dear friends who are lost and wandering...hear me. Send me a sign."

The crowd started to whisper and point up at the windows. From the corner of her eye, Leila thought she saw movement behind some of the panes without curtains, but when she looked fully, she realized the windows were empty. Chills tickled her whole body.

"It is a truth, universally acknowledged," Sandra said, "that we create a home where we feel the greatest safety, the greatest comfort. And so it follows that the spirits might think of this hotel as their home. I don't blame them. Who among us would like to never leave the Grand Oak?" The crowd laughed, and several hands shot up. "But in order for this wonderful hotel to continue with business as usual, I must ask these troublesome spirits to consider moving on."

At once, some of the windows overlooking the rear patio began to shake and rattle in their frames. A murmur rose among the crowd, and Leila's jaw dropped in awe.

Ridley looked up at the building, one eyebrow raised, as if she was trying to figure out Sandra's trick. Leila wanted to believe it was real. If it was a trick, it was a well-planned one.

"Don't be angry!" Sandra shouted, throwing back her head, as if in thrall to the spirit world. "This is for your own good! Find your light in the darkness." The windows rattled even harder. "Walk on! Step into the glow! Into the warmth! Find your loved ones there! They will help you create your new home!"

Several flares flashed behind the darkened windows. The crowd screamed. And Sandra shuddered, flinging herself to the ground in the center of the Misfit circle, landing on her hands and knees. The kids gave her space, as if she too might burst into a bright white light.

There was a long moment where Sandra shook as though she were experiencing a personal earthquake. Leila was on the verge of stopping the séance, but Sandra raised her hand, asking her to wait.

A moment later, Sandra calmed. She lifted her head. Her face looked slack, exhausted. She stood and brushed herself off, then turned to look up at the abandoned wing. "They heeded my plea," she told her audience. "Your hotel is now ghost-free!"

The crowd began to cheer. Theo and the Golden twins clapped vigorously, but not as much as Leila, who clapped the hardest.

The applause ended when an angry voice called out from the back of the patio, "What is the meaning of all this?!"

TWELVE

The crowd parted and a small man in a white suit stepped forward. Leila recognized the hotel's manager immediately—Mr. Arnold. He wore his dark hair parted precisely down the center of his scalp. His face always boiled red, even when he wasn't angry. He looked around at the members of his staff who were standing in the crowd. They glanced down and spread out, trying to avoid his gaze.

"Well?!" he demanded. "What is this?"

"Hi, Mr. Arnold," said Izzy, waving as if she could simply shoo away his temper with a flick of her wrist.

"Madame Esmeralda was doing a séance to get rid of the ghosts that were haunting the rear wing of the lodge. She's incredible!"

"Ghosts? Who said anything about ghosts?" Mr. Arnold scanned the crowd, making sure that none of the guests appeared disturbed.

"Madame Esmeralda is actually quite famous," said Theo. "She performs all across the country. In front of huge crowds!"

The hotel guests who'd been watching let out a cheer. Mr. Arnold seemed to bask in the applause, as if he were the one who'd just done something incredible. Several women approached Sandra and asked her if she would be "performing" again before the end of the weekend. A couple others inquired about private readings. Sandra reached into her sleeve and handed them what looked like business cards. After seeing these interactions, the manager's expression changed from shock and frustration to smooth gratitude.

He shook Sandra's hand. "It just so happens that our headliner two nights from now has canceled," Mr. Arnold whispered to her. "I would be honored if you would fill in."

Sandra beamed. "I'd be thrilled!"

Mr. Arnold clapped his hands. "Wonderful!" he exclaimed. "I'll have my team start advertising the show immediately. After what you did just now and the way people talk in this town, the house is sure to be packed." With a wide grin, he turned and engaged with the resort guests.

"This is so exciting!" said Leila. "We get to see you on stage here at the Grand Oak!"

"It all worked out perfectly," said Theo.

"And I have *you* to thank," Sandra said to the Misfits. "Seems to me as though you six might just be better at this than my agent! Well then, if I'm to put together a show, I'd better start getting prepared. See you all very soon!" And with that, she twirled her caftan and started back up the path toward the main entrance.

"What just happened?" Ridley asked, looking baffled.

"Magic?" asked Carter.

Ridley went on, "But should we believe it? I have my doubts."

Leila smacked her lips. "Right now, I *believe* that I'm really thirsty. Let's go see Poppa in the kitchen. I can't *wait* to tell him what just happened."

"Oops!" Olly cried. One of the mice had crawled out of his vest pocket and scrambled up to his shoulder.

"Gotcha!" said Izzy, snatching up the rodent and cradling it like a baby. The other mouse peeked out of Izzy's vest pocket as if to see what was going on. "Look how adorable they are! Maybe the Other Mr. Vernon can give them some water too."

"I think we should call them Ozzy and Illy," said Ozzy....(I mean, *Olly*.)

"That might get confusing," said Illy....(I mean, *Izzy*.)

Izzy was correct. It *did* get confusing.

In the resort kitchen, the kids found the Other Mr. Vernon pouring what would become little chocolate soufflés into individual ramekins.

"Hey, Mr. V," Carter said. "Could we have some lemonade?"

"Of course, help yourselves."

"Poppa!" Leila practically shouted as she hugged her father. "You'll never guess what just happened!"

"You are absolutely correct," he said with a tilt of his chef's hat. "But I hope you'll tell me."

Words burst forth from Leila's mouth. As she told him about the events of the last hour, Carter poured everyone glasses of ice-cold lemonade. When Leila finished her story, her poppa looked impressed. He enveloped her in a great big bear hug. "Sandra must be so pleased. I bet she'll save you the best seats in the house."

"I am intrigued to see what else she can do," said Theo.

"But let's talk about what she *did* do," said Ridley.

"Or do did!" said Olly.

"*Doo-did-skee-bop-a-diddle-doodle-doo!*" Izzy improvised.

Ridley rolled her eyes at the twins, and they quieted, suddenly interested in what was in their vest pockets. "There were a bunch of flashing lights behind the curtains," said Ridley. "Don't you think she could've controlled those somehow, with, *I don't know*, electricity?"

"I'll bet she had some helpers," said Carter.

"But who?" asked Leila. "Sandra didn't say anything about bringing a whole group of people to Mineral Wells with her."

"Perhaps Sandra set it all up herself," Theo suggested. "I imagine she could have used ropes or maybe wires to manipulate the windows."

Though Leila usually loved debunking tricksters

and questioning illusions, she found herself getting strangely aggravated. Sandra was so worldly and fashionable and fun; Leila wished the Misfits would give her the benefit of their doubts. Leila found herself on the edge of telling her friends to stop it, when the Other Mr. Vernon said, "What are those?!"

He pointed his spoon at the mouse noses peeking out from Olly's and Izzy's pockets. "Um...certainly not mice," Olly said.

"Out of my kitchen!" the Other Mr. Vernon demanded. "I love you kids, but you have *health-code violation* written all over your new pocket friends. Out, please!"

"Thanks for the lemonade," Carter said, pushing Olly and Izzy toward the exit.

"Love you, Poppa," Leila added, following the group to the lounge area beyond the kitchen doors.

"Bad, Ozzy and Illy!" Olly said. "No cheese for you!"

"Come on, let's get our mice back home. We have rehearsal," Izzy noted.

"And the rest of us should get going too," Ridley said. "I have a new trick at home that needs my attention."

As the kids moved through the lounge, Leila saw that the tall-backed, pleated leather chairs and dense, dark-wood side tables were arranged into small seating areas. Moose, deer, and bear head trophies hung from the walls. Enormous potted palms, ferns, fiddle-leaf fig trees, and birds of paradise plants greened up the space, giving privacy to the people who were seated, reading newspapers or huddling together in hushed conversation. When she'd first come to Mineral Wells, Leila would play alone in this room, hiding among the grand plants, pretending the animal trophies were hunting her and she needed to be sneaky enough to escape from them. She smiled at the happy memory.

The Misfits were almost at the exit when the sound of Sandra's voice came from somewhere nearby, stopping Leila in her tracks. "Sandra's still down here," she said.

"Where?" Ridley asked. "I don't see her."

"There," said Carter, pointing to a far corner of the lounge.

The woman sat by herself in one of the leather chairs, wearing a worried expression. She was leaning backward as if trying to hide among the leaves of one of the giant decorative plants.

Leila corralled the group behind a wide column. "What's wrong with her?" she asked. "Do you think she's all right?"

"She seems to be talking to herself," said Theo.

"What's she saying, though? Do you think she's still trying to communicate with the hotel's ghosts?"

Ridley sighed. "There are lots of reasons she might be talking to herself. Maybe she's running through her stage performance in her head. Maybe she's thinking of supplies she'll need. Maybe she's just insane."

"That's not nice, Ridley," Leila said.

"I never said I was nice," Ridley said with a wicked little smile.

"Izzy and I talk to ourselves all the time," said Olly. "And we're perfectly normal."

"We're also normally perfect," Izzy added with a tap-dance flourish. "Well, *I* am at least."

From the privacy of her leather chair, Sandra hissed at seemingly no one. *"Absolutely not! I won't do it!"*

Peering around the column, Leila could see the woman's face turning red. Sandra was about to burst into tears. Leila stepped forward and rushed over, calling out to Sandra, "Is everything okay?"

Flustered, Sandra scrambled to her feet. "Leila! What are you still doing here?"

Leila stammered. "I...I..." But nothing else would come out of her mouth.

"Everything is fine," said Sandra, her fearful expression melting away into a sad smile. "I need to go up to my room now. But I'll be in touch, okay? Make sure you tell Dante about the show. I'd hate for him to miss it."

"Uh, okay." When Leila blinked, she found that the woman was already racing away toward the lobby staircase.

The others came up quietly behind her. "What was that all about?" asked Theo.

Leila's cheeks flushed, but she forced a smile. "I'm not really sure."

★ ★ ★

That evening, Leila and Carter sat by the light of a long taper candle and drank sweet birch beer with Mr. Vernon in the parlor of the apartment. The sound of peeping tree frogs drifted in through the open windows as Carter told him about the day. Mr.

Vernon snapped his fingers absentmindedly at the flame, changing it from yellow to green to blue to red. Each time it changed, Carter gave a small cheer. Leila was in an uncharacteristically quiet mood.

Finally, she broke her silence. "Dad, did the Emerald Ring ever hang out at the Grand Oak Resort?"

Mr. Vernon seemed to consider how to answer. "We did, yes. Quite a bit actually, in the rear wing of the lodge, when it was still habitable. But eventually, we drifted apart."

"That's weird," said Carter. "Sandra didn't mention anything about that."

Leila wanted to ask her dad about the fire that Carter had neglected to bring up, but she was nervous that discussing the rumor would put a clamp on his sudden willingness to talk.

"It's not weird at all," Mr. Vernon said. "The best magicians know how to control their audience's attention. Whatever happened today—those tales of a haunting followed by a séance—happened because Sandra wanted them to."

"What do you mean?" asked Leila.

"Let me ask a question: When did the rumors of the ghosts at the Grand Oak begin?"

"Olly and Izzy said it was just recently," Carter answered.

"Interesting!" Mr. Vernon sipped from his glass.

"What's so interesting about that?" asked Leila.

Mr. Vernon licked at his mustache, as if he was pretending not to hear.

"I think what he's saying is that there's a connection between Sandra arriving at the Grand Oak and the rumors of the haunting starting up."

"That *is* a strange coincidence," said Mr. Vernon.

"But maybe it's *not* a coincidence. Right, Dad?"

The man with the curly white hair stared out the window, a smile creeping across his face. "My, my...it finally seems to be cooling off! Do you feel the breeze?"

Leila groaned. Her dad was doing the thing where he'd give her a tiny hint and then expect her to figure out exactly what was on his mind. "So you're saying that Sandra arranged all of it?"

Mr. Vernon finally faced her again. "Magicians' tricks can sometimes have very long setups before they pay off."

"Can you tell us anything more about your old club, Mr. Vernon?" Carter asked. "What did you guys do in your meetings? Who were your other friends?"

"Oh, we weren't so different from your own magic club." Mr. Vernon yawned and then stood up. "But it's already so late! I'm afraid any more stories would only bore you to sleep. If only there were a place in Mineral Wells where you could search for answers to your questions." He wandered into the kitchen to put his empty glass in the sink. Then he called out, "Good night!"

"A place in Mineral Wells?" Carter repeated to Leila.

"Another hint," she said, rolling her eyes, amused that her dad was so predictable...and also...not.

"It would be easier if he'd just tell us!" Carter said, laughing.

Leila raised her eyebrows. "We already know that Dante Vernon doesn't do *easy*."

And with that, the two gave each other a quick hug and went off to bed.

But they didn't go to sleep. Not right away. Leila could hear Carter knocking on the wall between their rooms. It followed a recognizable pattern. Ridley's Morse code homework.

His knocks came again:

—• ——— / ——• •••• ——— ••• — ••• /
•••• • •—• • / — ——— —• •• ——• •••• —

Leila clutched at her key, which was resting on her chest. She tapped on the wall beside her bed:

——• ——— ——— —•• / —• •• ——• •••• — /
—•—• •— •—• — • •—•

After that, his knocking stopped. And the sound of the tree frogs peeping from outside was like a lullaby, luring Leila to sleep.

THIRTEEN

I know, I know.... You're probably thinking: "Again with the superstition about the number thirteen?"

To that, I shall answer: Superstitions are not so easily eradicated. Who among you doesn't flinch when a black cat crosses your path? Do you avoid walking under ladders? And what about broken mirrors? Seven years can seem like eternity when dealing with bad luck!

Just like in the first book, I think it's best we skip this chapter. While I work on my fear of thirteen, why don't you enjoy a performance from Ridley's Top Hat?

That rabbit doesn't do much, does it? Other than wiggle its cute little nose, I mean. Great! Well, let's get back to it. Go on and turn the page....

FOURTEEN

After breakfast, Leila and Carter met up in the secret room at the back of the magic shop before it opened for the day.

"I was thinking," Leila whispered.

"Again?" Carter asked with a grin.

"Last night before bed, Dad mentioned that he and his friends would meet in the rear wing of the lodge. What if that was his roundabout way of saying, '*Go look there*'? We've wanted answers about his old club. The abandoned wing might be where we find them."

Carter nodded. "True. Even if that wasn't what he was saying, it's still worth an expedition."

"Let's call the others and see if they can meet us after Dad gets back from the grocery store," said Leila.

A knock sounded at the shop's front door. Leila and Carter leapt out from the secret room and closed the entry quietly. Leila came around the aisle and, to her surprise, found Sandra waving through the window. Her hair was pulled back in a wild ponytail, and she wore a soiled blue smock over a pair of dark jeans. The only indication that she was *the* Madame Esmeralda was her familiar white star-shaped earrings. Leila unlocked the door and let her in. "Good morning, my friends!" Sandra exclaimed.

"Hi, Sandra!" said Leila.

"Are you ready for your show?" asked Carter.

"I spent all last night going over my usual routine," said Sandra. "Today, I'm doing some cleanup at my house around the corner and thought I'd stop by to ask Leila an important question."

She removed a large deck of colorful cards from the pocket of her jeans and gave them a quick shuffle. Next, she spread them out on the counter in a fan shape before plucking one from the center and

turning it over. The image
on the card was unlike
any pictures Leila had
ever seen on her dad's
regular decks. Instead,
there was an elaborate
illustration   showing
a woman kneeling by a
natural pool underneath light

beaming down from seven stars overhead. The woman
on the card poured water from two jugs—one stream
fell into the pool, and the other fell onto the land.
"My tarot cards predict...that you will say...*yes!*"

"Shouldn't I hear the question first?" Leila asked.

"I suppose so." Sandra chuckled. "I would be honored if you would agree to be my opening act at the
Grand Theater."

Leila glanced at Carter, who stared back in surprise. "You want me to be your opening act?" She felt
faint. *Tomorrow night?*

Sandra nodded hopefully.

"Brilliant!" said Carter.

"But why me?" asked Leila. "Why not the other
Misfits?"

"We won't have time for everyone to show off their skills. But you are talented and enthusiastic, and I think you'll be great. Don't you think Dante will adore seeing you on stage?"

"I hope so," Leila answered, her voice wobbling.

"Don't worry," said Carter. "I'll give you tips on how to work a crowd."

"She already knows how to do that," said Sandra. "She's Leila Vernon. She can do anything!"

Carter and Leila were sitting on the shop's floor, cutting up and tying pieces of rope together in preparation for Leila's first solo act. Mr. Vernon came through the front door, followed by Theo and Ridley.

"Look who I found wandering around outside," said Mr. Vernon.

"I don't know what we would have done if he hadn't come along," said Ridley.

"We might have gone on wandering forever," Theo added with his soft smile.

Mr. Vernon nodded at the knotted mess on the floor between Leila and Carter. "Are we planning on tying up several tiny people this morning?"

"Even better!" said Carter, nudging Leila. "Go on, tell him!"

Leila's face grew red. "Sandra stopped by and asked me to be her opening act tomorrow night at the Grand Oak."

"Awesome!" Ridley yelled with a raised fist.

"Congratulations, Leila," said Theo. "You deserve it, most assuredly."

Mr. Vernon knelt down and wrapped his arms around her, giving her a warm squeeze. "That is truly spectacular, honey," he whispered into her ear.

"We've been trying to figure out how her act should go," said Carter. He snapped his fingers and a pair of thumb cuffs appeared in his hand. "I suggested using these."

Leila took the device from him, snapped the tiny cuffs around her thumbs, and held up her hands to show the others. "I don't think the effect will be big enough for the Grand Oak stage." She wriggled her fingers and the cuffs fell to the floor with a clatter. "See? Not impressive."

"*I* am impressed," Theo said, examining the small cuffs.

Leila glanced at Mr. Vernon. "I was hoping that Dad would teach us how to do the amazing escape act that I saw him do on the day I met him. The one with the assistants in masks, and the oil-cloth hood."

"That one took my friends and me months of practice," said Mr. Vernon.

Leila's grin hid her disappointment. "You'll teach me one day, won't you?"

"Of course! When we have more time."

"Sandra says the show starts at eight o'clock tomorrow. You'll be there—right, Dad?"

Mr. Vernon frowned. "I'm sorry, honey. I have some very important business at the store at that time."

Leila couldn't believe her ears. "More important than my first solo act? I'm going to be on stage by myself at the Grand Theater. And Sandra really wants you to be there."

"I'm sure Sandra does," Mr. Vernon answered. "But your poppa will come. And all your friends. You'll have oodles of support. The whole town!"

"I don't want the whole town! I want you!"

"In that case," said Mr. Vernon, perking up even more, "we'll have a Vernon's Magic Shop exclusive after you get home." He waved a showman's flourish. "*Leila's Encore!* How about that?" Leila's face fell. Immediately, Mr. Vernon softened, leaning closer to her. "I am so, so sorry. If there was any other way...but there's not. I'll make it up to you. *I promise*."

He held out his hand, and a bouquet of pink feather flowers appeared in a blink. Though she took them from him, she couldn't help but pay for them with a sad smile.

FIFTEEN

After they'd spent most of the day preparing for her act, Carter dragged Leila out of the shop for a well-deserved break. "Where are we going?" she asked.

"To the Grand Oak Resort to meet our friends," Carter answered with a sly smile.

Theo and Ridley were on the back patio. Now they just waited for Olly and Izzy to arrive. Late-afternoon light streamed through the trees, tossing dappled shadows against the walls of the building. Leila thought of the strange lights that she'd seen in the windows during Madame Esmeralda's séance. Together, the four Misfits guessed at what they might find inside the old building. Ridley perched eagerly forward in her chair, staring at the door of the abandoned wing. It was open a crack. A sliver of shadow stared back at them.

"That bellhop must have forgotten to lock up yesterday," Ridley noted.

"Or maybe a ghost unlocked it for us," Theo said.

"I'm not sure I believe in ghosts," Leila said, "but there's still something about this old place that gives me the chills."

"Me too," said Theo.

"Me three," Carter added with a grin. "We're not here to investigate ghosts today, though. We're here to learn more about the Emerald Ring. Let's tuck the supernatural concerns away for now."

Once more, Leila clutched the key at her chest. It felt good to have something to hold on to. The key grounded her, as did having her friends at her side.

"*Always together*," a voice said into her ear.

"*Never apart*," added another voice at her other ear.

Leila wasn't sure which way to spin. But when she

did turn, she found that Olly and Izzy had crept up on the rest of the Misfits, as they tended to do.

"Where is Madame Esmeralda?" asked Olly, holding up one of the field mice.

Izzy held up her own mouse, adding, "We wanted to show her the trick we taught Ozzy and Illy."

"I thought it was *Olly and Izzy*," said Ridley, scrunching up her forehead.

"That's us," said Izzy. "*These guys* are Ozzy and Illy."

"Sandra's in the auditorium prepping for the show," Leila interrupted, before the conversation could grow any more exasperating.

"We're so excited for you!" said Olly.

"Congratulations, Leila!" said Izzy. "It's a huge deal to be an opening act at the Grand Theater. Think of the openers who've warmed up audiences for all the great performers over the years!"

Ridley looked curious. "Like who?"

Olly and Izzy glanced at each other, then shrugged.

"Well, thank you." Leila bowed graciously.

"What is the trick?" Theo asked the twins, nodding at the mice.

"Oh, right." Olly presented his mouse again. Izzy

held her mouse up beside his. He waggled his fingers at the two rodents. "I've hypnotized them both to *stop speaking*!" Everyone waited. The mice did nothing but sniff at the air between them.

"They're fast learners," said Izzy.

"So impressive!" said Olly. "Aren't they?"

"Do you *really* want to know the answer to that?" asked Ridley.

Olly and Izzy shook their heads. They were used to receiving critiques about their performances, but not from Ridley.

(Friends, take note: Sometimes, your audience isn't going to respond the way you'd like them to. Most times, you can't escape by running off stage and hiding, so it's a good idea to learn to let words roll off you, like water off a duck's back.)

Ridley sighed. "Okay, now that *that's* over with, who's ready to explore?"

"If the door is already unlocked, is it wrong to enter?" Leila wondered aloud as she pushed the door open. It creaked all the way until it finally stopped, and the building beckoned the children to enter.

"That's *debatable*," said Carter, walking in first. The

others followed. "I'll ask my uncle, the criminal, the next time I see him—which, I hope, is *never*."

The entryway was filled with junk—bags of cement, broken lawn furniture, dusty croquet mallets, weathered rowboats and oars—all stacked up against the walls. This part of the hotel had been closed up for such a long time that every surface was coated in dust. "Look there," said Theo, pointing at the floor. "Footprints."

"Someone's been in here recently," Carter whispered.

"The bellhop did say they use this area for storage," Ridley recalled.

"At least the footprints are human," said Izzy. When the others gave her a funny look, she shrugged. "I didn't mean monsters. They could've been rabid raccoon tracks."

"Or coyote," Olly added.

"Or bear," Izzy went on.

"Or monkey!" said Carter.

The Misfits cleared a path to allow Ridley's chair to fit through, and then they made their way into the main hall. Several streaks of sunlight slanted across the space, dusty motes turning lazily in the beams. At the end of the hall, another door waited for them. This one, however, was chained shut.

Leila pushed forward. "This lock is nothing!" She pulled her tools from her pocket and got to work. In no time, the lock and chains were on the floor, and the Misfits were moving on. The next hallway was darker, packed with shadows and cobwebs and a musty smell that made everyone want to cough. Closed doors lined the hall on both sides.

"Did your dad mention *where* in the abandoned wing the Emerald Ring used to hang out?" Theo asked as they came to a staircase. One set of steps went up to the second floor; the other went down to a dark basement.

"Of course not," said Leila. "Dad never gives away the answer to anything unless he absolutely has to."

"Mr. Vernon is training us to think for ourselves," Carter added.

"Training is for animals," said Ridley. "I wish he'd spill the beans already!"

"I think we just need to look around a little bit," said Leila.

"Olly and Izzy, you check the rooms on that side of the hallway," Leila suggested. "Me and Ridley will explore this side. And Theo and Carter can keep a lookout at both ends."

"*Us?*" Theo and Carter spouted out at the same time.

"Unless you're scared," Leila teased.

"I can only speak for myself," said Theo. "The answer is *yes*. But that does not mean I will shy away from it. Neither shall Carter."

Carter cringed. "Right."

"Okay, then," said Ridley. "Let's meet out here in ten minutes. Or just holler if you find anything."

"But be sure to scream if you see a ghost," said Leila.

"Silly," said Izzy. "Madame Esmeralda got rid of all the ghosts yesterday!" When no one said anything, she added, "*Didn't she?*"

Leila and Ridley went door to door, peering into the shadowed rooms. Most were empty. In a couple, there was wallpaper hanging from the walls in great, droopy strips. Some rooms had furniture piled up in corners, and rugs were rolled and stacked in others. Except for a trail of dusty footprints that led down the hallway, everything looked like it hadn't been touched in decades.

Ridley took Leila's wrist and stopped her from

opening another door. "You've been acting strange this week. I'm worried about you."

Leila tried to play it off. "Strange? In what way?"

Ridley held out her hand for Leila to shake. Leila grasped it, wondering what trick her friend had up her sleeve. After Ridley let go, Leila glanced at her palm: The word *strange* had appeared in black ink on her skin.

"In *that* way," Ridley smirked. "But seriously, is everything okay?"

Leila laughed. "I have no idea what you're talking about."

"At first I figured that Bosso's monkey showing up at your place in the middle of the night was bugging you. But when I thought about it, I realized that something was wrong even before that. You haven't been yourself ever since the incident with the stolen diamond."

Leila found her hand drifting to the key on the string. "I guess it was kinda scary to see my favorite people in danger like that."

Ridley stared at Leila in silence for a couple seconds, then nodded. "Fair enough. Just know that if you ever need to talk, you know, about *anything*...I'm here for you. We all are. The Misfits, I mean."

"Oh, I know that, Ridley." Leila squeezed her friend's shoulder. "You didn't even need to say it."

"But that's the thing," Ridley replied. "I think that I did."

Leila knew Ridley was right. There was a lot about Leila's life she'd never told anyone in Mineral Wells, not even her fathers. She didn't want to make anyone feel bad for her. It was just easier to lock her old memories away and hide them behind a smile.

You see, the thing about smiling is that if you do it often enough, it can actually make you happier. Leila had learned this early on. It was one of her best tricks.

Ridley's concern touched Leila's heart. She might cry or confess everything to Ridley if she didn't do something. So she reached out and turned the doorknob. Peering into the darkness, she could make out framed posters hanging on the opposite wall. Names on the posters looked familiar. She'd seen them in books and on pictures that decorated Vernon's Magic Shop. *Thurston. Kellar. Houdini. Alexander: The Man Who Knows.*

"We found it!" Leila rushed into the room with Ridley just behind her. In the dim light, they stared at the old posters, which were advertisements for long-ago performances at the Grand Theater. Leila reached toward a window curtain to draw it aside and bring light into the room.

But Ridley cried, "Stop!" and Leila froze. "Someone outside might see us. I know the outer door was open, but I doubt the manager would be happy that we strolled right in. I have a better solution." Wheeling over to where Leila was standing, Ridley lowered her voice and said, "*Behold.*" Raising her right hand, she snapped her fingers. A flame floated a few inches above her pointer finger, providing just enough light for Leila to see by. Leila squeaked in surprise and then clapped.

By the flickering light of Ridley's finger, Leila noticed a dozen or more symbols carved into one portion of the wall. "Wow," Leila whispered. She ran her fingers over the carvings, as if she could read them that way. Many

of them were simply the suits from playing cards: diamonds, clubs, hearts, and spades. Inside a few of the
hearts, someone had carved what looked like initials:

"If these were left by the Emerald Ring," Leila wondered aloud, "what do K and A stand for?"

"I don't know," Ridley answered, "but a few of these
initials look like they were crossed out. Weird. Guess
someone had a bad breakup."

Leila considered the wall. "Or one person carved
the initials, and someone else crossed them out. And
the first person came back and carved them again.
And the other person came back and crossed them out
again."

"Hmm. If that's true, it could be one reason that

the magic club broke apart. *Love*." Ridley spoke that last word as if she were chewing a large mouthful of tripe stew.

"Do you think it could have turned into *hate*?" Leila asked, wondering what role her dad must have played in this old game.

Ridley sighed. "Love doesn't need to transform into anything other than itself in order for people to get hurt. At least, that's what I've gathered from reading my mom's novels. I've never been in love."

Leila snickered. "Me neither."

She glanced at the initials and the symbols, imagining the drama that must have unfolded in this very room. Had her dad and Carter's dad practiced their first magic tricks here? Had they argued about who should belong in the Emerald Ring, and who shouldn't? Could this be the room where the old club had broken apart?

"Look over here. These symbols are different." Just below the poster advertising a show featuring *Alexander: The Man Who Knows*, a few more carvings stood out. They were more detailed than the simple playing card suits. One looked like a stick with leaves growing from it. The second was a star inside a circle. Another looked like a chalice. The last symbol was half-hidden on the wall underneath the poster frame. Leila removed the poster, revealing the carving to be a sword.

"I've seen these before," said Leila.

Ridley's eyes lit up with recognition. "Wand, coin, cup, and sword," she said. "They're suits from a deck of cards. Tarot cards. Fortune-tellers use them to divine your future."

"Sandra brought over a pack this morning!" said Leila. "I think my dad keeps a couple tarot decks in his office. He doesn't use them. He just likes the illustrations."

"It would make sense, then, if Sandra carved these symbols here a long time ago," Ridley noted. "The question is: *Why?*"

Leila glanced down at the back of the poster and gasped. She turned the frame so Ridley could see the black ink scribbled onto the cardboard. It was a sentence. A *message*. Ridley leaned close as Leila crouched and sat on her heels.

Leila handed the poster to Ridley and went to the door, calling to the others, "Hey! We found something!" The Misfits all came running.

Noticing the carvings on the wall, Carter said, "Tarot

symbols." He glanced at Leila, seemingly remembering her divination from that morning. "Was Sandra here?"

"Once upon a time, perhaps."

They crowded around Ridley's chair and examined the writing on the back of the framed poster by the light of her finger's flame. Theo read the message aloud: "*Where Action Meets Thought, We Discover Reward.*"

"Seems like some sort of pledge," said Leila.

Ridley nodded. "Maybe it's a motto that the Emerald Ring once used to start their meetings."

"Or maybe it's a secret code," said Carter.

"Or a riddle," Izzy suggested.

"Oh, we just love riddles!" said Olly. "Right, Izzy?"

"Posi-tutely! Here's one: What was the psychic medium's secret hobby?"

"I know! I know!" said Olly. "She was a *ghostwriter!*"

"If it *is* a riddle," said Leila, "maybe Sandra left it here to point somebody toward something."

"Or some*one*," said Carter.

"Or some*where*," Theo added.

"Whatever it was pointing toward," said Leila, "I'll bet it's still here, somewhere in the abandoned wing."

"Even after all this time?" asked Ridley. "According to Dean the bellhop, there was that fire...." She wiggled her fingers and the flame sparked. "And then the water damage..." She shifted in her wheelchair, and a fine mist shot out from the handlebars, spraying the group. They flinched and jumped away as Ridley chuckled. "And then the termites." She moved her elbow, and one of the secret compartments sprang open, plastic bugs from Vernon's shop leaping out, making everyone jolt in surprise.

"Clever," said Carter, impressed.

Leila wouldn't be distracted. "It can't hurt to keep looking."

"We didn't find anything on the other side of the hallway," said Olly.

"Except for some mousetraps," said Izzy, "which I stayed far away from." She peeked into her pocket to make sure her mouse was safe and sound.

"There was a set of stairs at the end of the hallway," said Theo. "I think they lead down to a basement."

The Misfits looked at one another with fear in their faces. Carter spoke up. "If there's one thing I've learned, it's that the scariest places have the biggest reward."

"Reward," Leila echoed. "Just like *where action meets thought*. Come on, everyone. Follow me!"

SIXTEEN

Staring into the darkness from the top of the staircase, Theo asked, "Are you sure you all want to do this?"

"You're welcome to wait up here with me," said Ridley. "There's no way I can make it down these steps."

"We'll be quick," said Leila.

Carter removed his flashlight from his satchel. "You know, there are things other than ghosts that should make us nervous. So, everyone, be careful," he said, taking the first step down. Leila, Theo, and Olly crept slowly after him. Ridley and Izzy stayed behind.

At the bottom, Carter's flashlight swept across the stone floor below and the cobweb-covered rafters overhead. Leila could barely see. She heard the others trample down the steps behind her. Theo and Olly brushed against her on either side, clutching at her arms. It was so quiet that Leila could hear her friends breathing. She felt something pull against her ankle, like a string or a wire, and she nearly tripped.

But before she could check it out, something tall and pale appeared in the far corner. Leila gasped as Carter shone his light at it. Like something from a bad dream, *a human skeleton* jumped out!

Its arms and legs shivered and shook as it slowly moved toward her. Carter froze in his tracks, the light trembling in his hand. Olly and Theo shrieked, and Leila leapt away from them. The skeleton jittered forward, then to her surprise, it dropped in a heap to the floor.

From up the stairs, Ridley cried out, "Is everyone okay down there?"

Carter crept toward the pile of bones, keeping the light steady. Leila gulped down a hard knob that had moved into her esophagus; she was worried that the thing might jump up again and attack. "Wires," Carter whispered to himself. He reached out and grabbed what looked like fishing lines dangling down from a railing. Leila caught a glimpse of the light reflecting off them.

"How bizarre," said Theo.

A rail was attached to the rafters. Following the light, Leila noticed where the rail originated: a far corner of the space. Her face lit up like a bonfire when Carter shifted his beam and briefly blinded her.

"Hey!" Ridley shouted. "You guys are scaring us up here!"

"Don't worry yourselves," Leila called. "Just had a bit of a fright is all."

"I'll go get them," said Olly. He rushed back up the stairs.

Carter wandered toward the corner, exploring the spot where the skeleton had come from. Leila raced over to him, not wanting to be left in the dark.

"What is it?" said Ridley, edging down the stairs in her chair with Olly and Izzy's help, step by careful step.

"A booby trap," said Theo, staring up at the rail. "Someone rigged up a trip wire and a fake skeleton. There is probably a hidden system of pulleys somewhere nearby. Over time, the wires must have decayed. That is why it fell to the floor."

"But why set up a booby trap?" Olly asked, reaching into his pocket and pulling out his mouse. He nuzzled it with his nose.

Izzy nudged his shoulder. "Obviously, it was to trap a booby!"

Carter laughed. "No, they did it to scare people away. A classic trick."

"Was this before or after the fire, the flood, the mold, and the infestation?" Ridley asked.

"I'm sure my dad would know," said Leila. "I

wonder what they were trying to scare people away from."

"Pirate treasure," said Izzy. "That's usually what dancing skeletons are for."

"Mineral Wells is landlocked, silly." Ridley scoffed, and she rolled across the bumpy stone floor. "Would've been kind of difficult for pirates to get up through these hills to us landlubbers, don't you think?"

"Maybe the Emerald Ring was trying to scare people away from this corner," said Carter, who was focusing on the floor and the basement walls near where he was standing. There didn't seem to be anything remarkable about the spot; the stones there were smooth and grouted with old, crumbly cement.

"But we all know that magicians are about *misdirection*," Leila stated. "I doubt Sandra or the others in the old club would have set up a trap that pointed directly to the place they were trying to keep secret." She nodded at the track that ran across the ceiling, the path that the skeleton had danced along. "More likely, they'd choose the other side of the room."

Curious, Carter shone his light at the opposite

corner. To Leila's surprise, the stones in the floor over there looked different—they had white markings on them. Together, the Magic Misfits rushed to check them out.

In the center of each stone was a faint image drawn in chalk. Leila gasped. "These are the symbols from the tarot deck," she said. "Just like the ones carved into the wall upstairs."

Ridley pushed through the others to get a better view. "Leila's right. The suits—swords, cups, coins, and wands." Every stone in this particular corner was marked with one of the small icons. They practically glowed under the flashlight beam.

"You think Sandra did this?" Carter asked.

"Maybe," Leila answered, uncertain.

"Why here?" Theo studied the floor. "What is the significance?"

"The riddle," Ridley whispered. *"Where action meets thought, we discover reward."*

"Reward!" said Izzy.

"Wow, we found it," said Olly. "We're rich!"

"Flat-out, stinking rich!" Izzy did a little tap dance. "I'm gonna get a pony! And a pony for Illy."

Olly's eyes went wide as his imagination went wild. "And I'm gonna buy the world's biggest ice-cream sundae. And a new mouse house for Ozzy!"

Leila shook her head. "We have to figure out what it means first. Ridley, what else do you know about the tarot symbols?"

"Way too much for me to remember right now," Ridley said. "I do know that the symbols on these stones are connected to the suits on playing cards. Coins are like diamonds, representing wealth or security. Wands are like clubs, symbols of action and inspiration. Cups are hearts, vessels that can be full or empty. And swords equate to spades— sharp tools that cut and divide like thought and analysis, helping us reach the secret center of what we desire."

Theo gasped, smacking his fist into his palm. "That's it!" He glanced at the others. "Ridley just said it herself. Wands are like clubs. *Action.* Swords are like spades. *Thought.* Where *action* meets *thought*!"

"We need to find a stone marked with both a wand and a sword," said Leila.

Carter handed the flashlight to Ridley, and the rest of the Misfits got down on their hands and knees to search.

Leila knelt by a stone where the image of a wooden wand crossed the image of a gleaming sword. "I found it!"

SEVENTEEN

The others crowded around as Leila shoved her fingers into a small space along one edge. She grunted as she lifted the corner of the stone. It slipped out of place, revealing a shallow hole just below.

"Whoa!" Carter exclaimed. Ridley's jaw dropped in shock. Theo shouted, "Yes!" Olly and Izzy locked elbows and did a quick spin around each other.

"Reward," Leila whispered. Ridley shone the flashlight into the hole. A small wooden box sat snugly beside a metal box. Leila reached in and pulled them both out. She wasn't thinking about *reward* in the same way as the twins. She was hoping to find what she'd come in here for. *Answers to her questions about who her father and his friends used to be.* As she placed the wooden box on the floor beside her, Carter said, "It kinda looks like my puzzle box. The one with my father's initials."

"This one has initials too," said Theo. "AIS."

"Who is AIS?" asked Carter.

"Maybe the same person whose initials were carved into the wall upstairs," said Ridley. "Or at least *one* of them: *A.*"

"Weird," said Leila. "I wonder what's inside this thing." She tried to open it but the lid wouldn't budge.

"I could never figure out how to open my dad's box either," Carter explained.

"Maybe all the members of the Ring had impossible boxes like this," Theo suggested.

"Try the metal one instead," Ridley insisted.

To Leila's surprise and delight, the metal lid squeaked open. She reached in and pulled out a folded, yellowing piece of paper. She opened it up and showed the others. Rough black lines squiggled around the page. Several *X*s were marked on the lines. And beside each *X* were strange letters.

"It looks like a map—except all weird," said Leila.

"A map of what, though?" Ridley asked.

As the others pored over the map, Leila noticed Carter examining the wooden puzzle box. It was so like his own—the one which once belonged to his father. He slipped it into his satchel for safekeeping.

"Maybe the letters are another riddle," Theo suggested.

"Or a *cipher*," said Ridley. She reached into her wheelchair's secret compartment and retrieved the coin that had fallen out of the air at the magic shop. She examined it. Two rings, one inside the other, each contained all the letters of the alphabet. Every letter in the inner ring matched up with a letter in the outer ring. "And here's what we can use to decode it. We just switch out the letters for their corresponding counterparts."

"Whoa," said Carter. "This is crazy!"

"It's simpler than it looks." Ridley produced a pencil from her wheelchair's arm and started decoding. "Check this out." She showed the others her work.

T.L.I. = G.O.R.   E.N.H. = V.M.S.

"It still makes no sense," Theo said with a sigh.

"Maybe they're just initials," said Olly.

"G.O.R.," said Izzy. "Grand Oak Resort?"

Ridley laughed. "Olly, Izzy, you're geniuses!"

"Thanks!" said Olly. "Most people compliment our smiles, so it's nice to hear that you like our brains too."

Ridley rolled her eyes. "I wouldn't go that far. But I was right to ask everyone to study Morse code! See? Secret clubs use secret codes!"

(Yes, friends, Ridley was right! And the cipher that the Magic Misfits discovered was a substitution cipher called Atbash. This cipher has a long history. It's been used by secret clubs and societies all around the world. Maybe you've already encountered the cipher in this very book....Hmm, I wonder where. If you're ever feeling secretive, you might try using Atbash to send encrypted messages to people you know—people like your little brother or sister, or maybe your mom or dad or teacher. Who knows? They might be clever enough to figure it out all by themselves!)

"So then it *is* a map," said Carter, pointing at the page. He placed his finger on one of the *X*s and traced the line to the next *X*. Glancing at the cipher, he said,

"The Grand Oak Resort. V.M.S." After a second, he cried out, "Vernon's Magic Shop!" Then he scowled. "But these lines don't look anything like the roads around Mineral Wells."

Leila pointed to the corner of the map. "What's this jumble of letters say? Can I see the cipher coin so I can decode it?"

Quickly, she replaced the coded letters with the real ones. Her eyes went wide with surprise. "They're not roads after all. They're"—she read the words—"*bootlegging tunnels*."

"What are bootlegging tunnels?" asked Carter.

"Ooh, I know!" Ridley spoke up.

"Of course you do," Theo teased.

Ridley scowled at him, but continued, "Back during the era of Prohibition, the production, transportation, and sale of alcohol was a federal crime. So smugglers—called bootleggers—had to do it in secret. Folks skirted the law by serving alcohol to customers in secret clubs called speakeasies."

"A secret club like ours?" asked Izzy.

"Not exactly," Theo said.

Ridley went on, "To get the cases of alcohol inside these speakeasies without the authorities noticing, oftentimes the bootleggers would dig secret passages, connecting the sites with an intricate tunnel system."

"Secret passages." Carter considered. "Like the bookcase at the back of the magic shop! Hey, I wonder if Mr. Vernon's place was once an old speakeasy."

"Remember what Poppa said? It used to be a jazz club!" Leila said.

"There must be an entrance to the tunnel system here too," Theo surmised. "GOR. Grand Oak Resort. Right?"

Leila nodded. She refolded the map and handed it to Carter, who tucked it into his satchel. "This feels important. Let's look around. Carter, take your flashlight to that side of the basement. And Ridley can use her secret fire-finger to illuminate this side."

"Be careful not to set off any booby traps this time." Ridley winked.

The group split in two and started to explore. Soon, Carter's flashlight beam settled on a tall, rusted door embedded in the wall behind the staircase. "This must be it!" He shoved his shoulder against the door, but it wouldn't budge.

"There's a keyhole," said Ridley. "What's that strange emblem marked just above it?"

Since Leila was the lock expert, she leaned close to the hole and examined it. When she saw the emblem, her body went numb. It was the same exact shape as the design on the key she was wearing around her neck!

She knew what she had to do, but she'd never told the others about the key. Would her friends be mad at her for keeping it to herself? Would she be mad at herself for finally revealing one of her most precious secrets—the one that always reminded her where she'd come from?

She reached into her shirt, removed the key, and showed it to the Misfits. They all gasped.

"Where'd you get that?" asked Carter.

"I've had it ever since I can remember. Someone left it in my bassinet on the steps of Mother Margaret's Home. I've never told anyone. Not even Poppa or Dad," said Leila, her stomach fluttering as if filled with a hundred butterflies. She waited for their responses, for Ridley to scowl at her, for Theo to look hurt that she'd never shown him before. Instead, they rallied around her, giving her a hug.

"Thank you for telling us," Carter said.

"Now see if it fits," said Ridley, her voice hushed with anticipation.

Had Leila been worried all this time for nothing? The others looked over her shoulders as she inserted the key into the hole. It fit perfectly. She tried to give it a turn, but the key wouldn't budge. Her disappointment felt like the shock of a pick against a block of solid ice. Wounded, she couldn't keep her voice from wavering. "I really thought that would work."

Ridley smacked her arm lightly. "Since when has a tough lock ever stopped Leila Vernon?"

Trying to hide her frustration, Leila reached into her pocket and removed her lucky lock-picks. She fiddled with them at the rusted door, turning and spinning and snagging at the impossible contraption inside, but it was no use. This lock appeared to be one of the most sophisticated she'd ever encountered. "If I keep it up," she said, "I might damage my tools.... And then I'd have to rethink my plans for the show tomorrow."

"Speaking of which," said Ridley, "didn't you agree to practice with your dad for the performance tomorrow?"

Leila looked at her watch. "Oh no. I'm gonna be late."

"And I'm about ready to be out of this basement,"

Carter said. "Shall we all head back?" Everyone agreed they'd had enough excitement for one day. They could come back and solve the mystery of the bootlegging door soon.

As she climbed the stairs, Leila remembered what Sandra had told her at dinner the other night. The psychic reading felt like a prophecy now. *This key will become important in the coming days. Keep it close.* Feeling suddenly woozy, she grasped at the wall to keep from falling backward.

EIGHTEEN

The sun was dipping behind the bigger hills in the west as Theo and Ridley accompanied Leila and Carter up to the resort before the show. Leila tried not to focus on her dad's absence, especially because her friends and Poppa would be present. To ease her anxiety, the group stopped at the resort's kitchen. The Other Mr. Vernon gave her a warm hug and said, "You'll be amazing tonight."

The quartet found Izzy and Olly waiting for them in the lobby, then together, the Misfits walked to the theater. They took the talent entrance, went downstairs to the snaking hallways under the stage, and located one of the large communal rooms where grand orchestras and choruses would prepare for the bigger shows. It was a perfect spot for Leila to rehearse one last time. She took a deep breath and said, "Let's get down to business."

As she finished tying together fake knots and pasting patches of fake skin onto her forearms (to cover up her special lockpicks), Leila's mind raced back through everything they'd discovered about the Emerald Ring in the abandoned wing. The riddle written on the poster had been intriguing, the skeleton both terrifying and silly, the symbols on the stones mysterious, the boxes and code and tunnel map surprising, and the secret door and impossible lock a bit shocking. Put them all together and they seemed to hint at a conspiracy that made Leila's gut ache. Sometimes, it felt safer to *not* have all the answers. Yet she understood that if she took that stance, she'd be left with her butt pointed toward the sky, and anyone walking by could kick it.

That wouldn't feel safe either.

What *did* make her feel safe was running through her escape act one final time with her friends.

A knock sounded at the door, and Sandra peeked in. She wore a brightly patterned floor-length caftan, her hair was tucked underneath a spangled purple turban, and her makeup made her look like a lioness. "Hello, everyone," she said. "Are we excited?"

The others nodded while Leila mustered up as much enthusiasm as she could. "Hi there," she said, cringing when her voice came out sounding shrill and terrified.

"Sorry for only now checking in." Sandra sighed. "It's been a hectic day, dealing with other people's wants. Is everybody ready?"

"We're getting there," said Ridley.

"How about you?" Theo asked Sandra.

"All this theater stuff is old hat to a dame like me. I can read minds with my hands tied behind my back. In fact, I may do just that." Sandra seemed to notice Leila's dour mood. "What is it, Leila?"

"Poppa will be here, but Dad can't make it. He has extra work at the store tonight."

Sandra's face slackened. "But he *has* to be here! It's your first real show!"

"I know," Leila said.

"Well, I don't mean to make you feel worse."

Sandra clicked her tongue. "Let me give him a call." She walked toward a black rotary phone sitting on a desk in one corner of the room.

"Really?" Leila said. "You'd do that?"

"Of course," Sandra said. She plucked the receiver from the cradle and dialed the store's number. The Misfits listened in on Sandra's half of the conversation:

"Dante? Hello, dear!...Yes, yes...We're all together in the rehearsal room at the theater. Listen, Leila tells me...That's right! Oh, I'm surprised at you!...You simply must come up, Dante, and that's an absolute fact. Just for a little while, for your daughter...Nonsense! Everything can be rearranged!" Sandra listened and continued to smile, but the light went out of her eyes and her voice changed, growing softer as if she was desperate to get through to him. "If you won't do it as a favor to an old friend, do it for Leila, Dante. Please?"

Leila watched as Sandra's smile dropped. She tried to imagine what her dad could possibly have said to make Sandra look that way.

Sandra turned toward the wall so none of the kids could see her face. Now she was whispering. "Dante, listen, I'm begging you. You have no idea how important—" Surprised, she held the receiver away from her ear and said, "Hello? Dante?" She pressed the phone switch several times. When she finally faced the Misfits, Sandra put on a forced display of acceptance. "We must have gotten disconnected. I'm sorry, Leila. He was adamant. I did try, though."

"I appreciate it," Leila said. "There will always be next time."

"That's the spirit!" said Sandra, returning to her former spunky self. "*Spirit!* Ha-ha! There should be plenty lurking about this evening. I'll tell them you say hello. Now I must be off to tend to last-minute matters." She gave a quick wave, then closed the door behind her.

★ ★ ★

The stage manager knocked on the door and entered. "You've got a big crowd out there tonight! Five minutes 'til curtain. Okay?"

"You're shaking," Ridley noted to Leila.

"I'm nervous," Leila said.

"You've got this," Carter said. "When you get on stage, imagine yourself back home at the magic shop, doing your escape act for just your dads."

"For once, Carter's right," Ridley added. "Think

of Mr. Vernon holding up a timer as you beat your record for getting out of the straitjacket. That's how you'll make it through these jitters."

Carter clasped Leila's arm. "You're going to do great. We'll be right beside you."

"I know you will." Leila smiled, trying to shake off the bad feeling. She glanced at her reassuring friends. "Thank you all." Her throat felt as if it were coated in sand, but she went on, "I just wanted to say that I'm sorry for being so...*strange* lately."

"There is no need to apologize to us," said Theo. "You only have to be yourself."

"That's the thing, though—my *usual* self is happy, supportive, and optimistic. I want to be all those things all the time. But recently, I've realized that I'm more than only those things. All the stuff boiling inside feels impossible to hide these days. I've tried to keep my past to myself, because it hurts to remember, and I don't want anyone to ever feel bad for me. That's why I never told you guys about my key. Or about some of the memories that keep my mind whirring on certain nights." Leila struggled to catch her breath. "I want to be the girl you've always known me to be...but some-times...sometimes, it's hard."

Ridley took her hand. "We know exactly who you are, Leila. And we love all your various parts...even the ones you think you've kept secret."

Leila chuckled nervously, and then her five friends gathered close and gave her a big group hug.

From down the hall, the stage manager called out to them, "You kids coming or what?"

NINETEEN

The Magic Misfits climbed the stairs and stood where the stage manager told them to. Across the stage, Leila could see Sandra waiting in the wings. Her eyes were closed, like she was concentrating. Peering around the edge of the curtain, Leila looked out at the enormous crowd. People filled seats from the front of the orchestra to the back, from the railing of the balcony all the way up to the nosebleed section. Poppa was directly in the center with a few of his cooks, all wearing their kitchen uniforms. Seeing him made her beam with calm. And when she took in the faces of her friends, she knew she'd be okay.

The lights dimmed, the curtain pulled upward, and the stage manager poked her in the shoulder. "Go on, kiddo!"

"I thought someone might introduce me," Leila whispered.

"Just introduce yourself, honey," the stage manager said, shooing her forward. "Everyone's going to love you."

A spotlight turned on, blinding her. Leila held up her hand so she could see, then realized she was blocking her face. She dropped her arms to her sides.

"Hello!" she cried out. She felt like her voice sounded as small as a mouse's, but she recalled the last time she was on this stage, when the stakes were much higher, as they took down Bosso and saved her father. She then thought of how hard it had been to tell her friends about her secret worries and fears, and she realized that she could definitely do this. In fact, she could do it with her eyes squeezed shut.

"My name is Leila Vernon!" Her voice was steady now. She noticed her friends standing in the wings.

She waved them toward her, and Carter, Theo, and the twins stumbled out into the stage lights, while Ridley rolled in her chair. "My friends and I have quite a show for you!"

The audience applauded politely. But then came one loud whoop and cheer, which Leila recognized as Poppa, and her heart swelled with love for him. At the same time, she wished her poppa and her dad were sitting, and cheering, together.

"First, a simple rope trick." She presented several pieces of white rope. The Magic Misfits helped her hold them up and stretch them across the stage. Then, with a quick snap of the rope, all the sections seemed to join together. The divided rope became whole!

The audience gasped, impressed that a group of kids was capable of something impossible. All the hours that she and Carter had spent practicing had been worth it. The sound of applause sent shivers down Leila's spine. She wanted to feel it again.

She called out, "Some folks say that girls like me should be quiet and polite. That we should mind our manners and speak only when spoken to. To these people, I'd ask that you watch this next trick closely and see what girls like me are capable of!"

A worried murmur fluttered through the auditorium, filling Leila with excitement.

Carter placed a chair in the center of the stage. Leila sat as Theo and Ridley very clearly tied her hands together in her lap. Then they wrapped another rope around her chest and the back of the chair so that it seemed she could barely move. Her friends then turned the chair around so that the crowd could see the knots that Leila had taught them to make. Ridley went so far as to tug on the ropes, and Leila grunted in what sounded like pain.

What the crowd didn't know was that while Theo and Ridley were tying her, Leila had been tensing her muscles and keeping her wrists wide apart. As they'd looped the coils around her chest, she'd inhaled as much breath as her lungs would allow, so that when it was time to escape, all she had to do was make herself smaller again.

Exhaling and relaxing, the ropes became loose around her, and Leila was able to slip out from inside them. In a blink, she was free, clutching the knotted bindings in her tight fists. She leapt up on the chair and did a little jig.

The audience loved it. And they loved *her*. Leila let their energy feed her. "Thank you!" she said with a bow, trying to keep her voice from shattering into a million giddy pieces.

"And now it's time for my big finale. One that is so impossible, *so claustrophobic*, you'll wonder if I've lost my mind for attempting it." From one of the wings, Carter and Theo had wheeled out a small trunk, only a little bit larger than a suitcase. From the other side of the stage, Olly and Izzy strolled out carrying Leila's bleached, white straitjacket, its long arms and buckles dragging across the floor.

When the audience saw these props, they grew frenzied with worry and excitement, talking to one another noisily.

The twins winked as they helped Leila get into the straitjacket. She reached across her chest, bringing her arms into an X shape. *Click-click-click*. The locks were in place now, and the jacket fit snugly, but not *too* snugly. She called out to the audience, "This time, I'll need a little help from all of you. If you would, as soon as the trunk is closed and locked with me inside it, please count me down from thirty."

Leila ducked into the trunk, the twins closed the lid, and the audience began counting down: "Thirty... twenty-nine...twenty-eight...!"

The other Misfits riled up the crowd, shouting, "Louder! Louder!" and "She can't hear you!" and "Go, Leila, go!"

"Twenty! Nineteen! Eighteen! Seventeen! Sixteen! Fifteen!"

Inside the box, Leila wiggled and worked to free herself. She listened to the audience as she methodically worked one arm loose. She raised it to her mouth and pulled the fake skin away, moving her lucky lock-picks between her lips before snatching them with her newly freed fingers. From there, she struggled to reach each of the locks that the twins had attached to the jacket. There was very little room for her to shift her body inside the trunk, but after years of practice, this feat had become one of her favorites to perform for her fathers back at the magic shop.

"Eleven! Ten! Nine!" But before the audience could say "Eight!" Leila popped out of the trunk. Everyone gasped in surprise. With a simple shimmy of her shoulders, the jacket slipped away, and she held up her arms in triumph.

The noise in the auditorium was more than Leila could have expected. Her eardrums rattled like casta-nets. She was so pleased she fought with all her might

to keep in the happy tears. She reached out for her friends and gathered them together for a final bow. Hopefully, this show would be the first of many.

Peering past the glare of the stage lights, she saw her poppa clapping ecstatically and waving to her. The sight of him filled her with rainbow reflections, sunny skies, memories of hot chocolate, and the warmest laughter in the whole world.

TWENTY

While the stagehands prepped the stage for the main act, the stage manager directed the kids to a group of open seats in the first row. Strangers kept patting Leila on the back and congratulating her. A few random kids even rushed up to her and asked, "Can we have your autograph?"

"Of course!" Leila agreed. "But only if my friends sign as well." The Misfits beamed as they passed the pens and paper around.

Soon, the auditorium lights dimmed and the

audience hushed. Madame Esmeralda's show was starting.

There were whispers in the row behind the Misfits about yesterday's séance:

"Did you see what that psychic did?"

"Those flashing lights were terrifying."

"She must be really special if she quieted those *ghosts*."

A voice boomed out, shocking everyone into silence. *"And now...please join the Grand Oak Resort in welcoming an illustrious talent to our stage. Guard your mind, steel your spirit, harden your nerves. Because you are about to encounter the world's most confounding clairvoyant...Madame Esmeralda!!!"*

From the darkened stage came a blast of noise and light and smoke, and then Madame Esmeralda appeared, walking out of a fog. Her smile lit up the room as she bowed, then she raised her arms in gratitude toward the crowd.

Her performance was as sleek and polished as crow feathers. She began by collecting little note cards on which audience volunteers had written statements about themselves. Reading through a few of them, she walked off the stage and moved through the aisles, the spotlight following her from above, surrounding her in a halo of chilly light.

To a red-haired woman, she said, "Your mother worked for a midwestern bank!"

To a tie-wearing man: "Your favorite color is mayonnaise white!"

To a teenage girl: "Your middle name is Anna-Rose!"

And to an old man of small stature: "You were once bitten by a shark near the island of Saint John."

Madame Esmeralda spoke to more and more people, and each of them stared at her in shock. "From the stunned looks on your faces," she called out, "it seems like I've struck some major chords." The crowd murmured, conferring with one another. "Was I correct?" Each of the volunteers stood and said, "Yes!" The audience burst into surprised applause, and the volunteers sat down again.

"For my next feat, we must all become a mite more mystical." She returned to the stage and removed a thin white candle from a pocket within her clothes. She dramatically struck a match. "Lights, please!" she called out to the people up in the theater booth. The stage lights faded into an overwhelming blackness. The candlelight flickered just below Madame Esmeralda's face, throwing spooky shadows across her features. She shouted, "I call upon the ancestors of this crowd to join us here tonight!" A hush fell over the audience. Then, growing subdued, Madame Esmeralda closed her eyes and whispered, "Be still!" With a small grin, she added, "Allow them to say hello."

From around the cavernous room, there came sudden shouts and cries of fear.

Someone called out, "It touched my neck!"

Another: "Something pinched my arm!"

Another person shrieked and shouted, "Its fingers are cold!"

Another: "My hair!"

And again: "My foot!"

Leila glanced around, wondering if one of the spirits might try to touch her too.

"Lights!" Madame Esmeralda proclaimed just as the audience seemed about to revolt and dash through the exit doors, fleeing into the hotel and out into the night. Her voice was a strong and steady comfort. "There is no reason to be scared. Spirits do not travel from the other side to hurt us. They're simply reminding us that they once lived here too.

"I shall now invite these spirits to speak through me!" The crowd grew restless again, talking among themselves. "But first, I need volunteers. If I point to you, please come up on stage with me." Madame Esmeralda randomly plucked seven people from all around the auditorium.

The seven stood in a line beside the psychic, each of them looking nervously into the glare of the stage lights. There was a stout, middle-aged woman wearing a stiff aqua gown; a taller, stooped gentleman in a pair of slacks, a white shirt, and a black tie; a very small boy dressed in a sailor outfit; and a girl, who was a bit taller than the boy beside her, wearing an A-shaped black-and-white polka-dot dress. A large man with broad shoulders wore a brown floor-length fur coat over a dark suit. (Leila thought this was odd, since it was so warm outside, but apparently he didn't like the air-conditioned atmosphere inside the auditorium.) His wire-rimmed glasses were oversize and completely round, and his long beard tickled the bottom of his collar.

Finally, beside him, a couple stood holding hands. The woman's red hair was coiffed in a high poodle-cut. The man was smaller than her, and on his head was an obvious black toupee that didn't match the

graying hair at his temples. They were dressed conservatively in a brown dress and brown suit. Their wide eyes were hopeful.

Something about these last two seemed familiar to

Leila. She racked her memory for where she might have met them before. Maybe they'd come into the magic shop this week. Had they been the ones who Presto had accosted with the strange message? Or had Leila seen them earlier than that? A long time ago...

TWENTY-ONE

"It shall work like this," Madame Esmeralda addressed her seven volunteers. "The spirits who have arrived will approach and secretly reveal details to me. I shall share these details one at a time with you. If at any point one of you feels that I am speaking about someone you've loved and lost, raise your hand and let me know. Okay?"

The small group nodded at the same time. Madame Esmeralda closed her eyes and began to hum, "*Ohmmmmmm.*"

After a few seconds, she held up a finger and then

pressed it directly into the center of her forehead. She blinked her eyes open wide, staring out above the audience as if she could see things floating there. "I see a woman. She is neither tall nor short. Her hair is long and brown. She wears an apron. I think...I think she works in a bakery. No. She *owns* the bakery." A hubbub rose from the audience, but none of the seven spoke up. "Her specialty was...rugelach. Her raspberry variety won the blue ribbon at a county fair....She's a kind person, a mother to two daughters....She was born overseas...Eastern Europe...and immigrated here as a teenager."

The stout woman in the aqua dress on the far left of the group waved her hand and shouted out, "That's my *bubbe*! There's no doubt about it!"

Madame Esmeralda strolled over to the woman and said, "Your bubbe says she misses you and loves you." The stout woman held her fingers to her lips as they quivered. Madame Esmeralda placed a comforting hand on her arm. "Do you ever hear birds singing inside your house?"

The stout woman's eyes flew open wide. "Yes, I do!"

"That is a sign your bubbe is there, visiting you."

"I can't believe it. How did you know so much about her?"

Madame Esmeralda answered with a smile. "She told me. She says to check behind your dresser in your bedroom. There, you will find something you've always treasured, but recently misplaced. Does this make sense?"

"Yes, it does! My wedding ring! Oh, thank you, Madame Esmeralda! I'll look as soon as I get home!"

By the time the stout woman sat back down in the auditorium, she was sniffling, and most of the audience was touched. The psychic turned to the six others left on stage. They stared back at her in awe and worry.

For the next twenty minutes, she described the spirits who were visiting the Grand Oak auditorium. "Here's a tall and handsome white man with silver hair and a long forehead." Or "A short brown woman with thick curls is smiling the grandest smile I've ever seen." If none of the volunteers spoke up, she would follow with additional information. "I sense the first name might begin with *F*. Or maybe *P*?" Or "This person was a descendant of someone from South America. I think...Uruguay?" And then something like "They were a machinist." Or "They walked with a cane." Or "I think this person might have been quite gassy," a statement that received as many gasps from the crowd as it did guffaws. As Madame Esmeralda gave more and more details about each spirit she was hearing from, eventually one of the volunteers would raise a hand. "That's my deceased wife!" exclaimed the slouching man in the overalls. "My grandfather!" the boy in the sailor suit blurted out. "My aunt Mabel!" shouted the girl in the A-shaped dress. "My cousin Gary," whispered the man in the fur coat.

Leila felt chills each time Sandra's predictions proved true, but the Misfits kept whispering around her.

"I bet she researched the histories of these people before the show," Ridley guessed.

"How?" Leila asked. "The show was too last-minute."

"If you think about it," said Theo, "she is doing exactly what she did for us during dinner the other night. She begins vaguely, luring the volunteers into admitting a connection that they might feel is tenuous at best."

"Ooh, *big* words!" said Izzy.

"I know some bigger words," Olly added. "Luminous. Magnanimous. Hippopotamus."

Leila shook her head. "And what about the bubbe

and the bakery? Sandra knew all that, and the woman said nothing."

"Good counterpoint," Theo replied.

"Maybe all these people on stage are working for her," Carter suggested.

"No, they're not," Leila answered, annoyed at herself for feeling exasperated.

"I think it's just easy for people to believe something is real when they need it to be," said Ridley.

"Exactly," Theo said.

"Believing in something doesn't make it automatically *not* real," Leila whispered.

Someone in the seats behind shushed them. Leila turned and quickly apologized. She thought back to when they'd all gone to Bosso's circus, and how Carter had taken them into a tent to speak with a woman called Madame Helga who'd told them, *Alone you are weak. Together you are strong.* Ridley had used the quote to help them learn Morse code. The experience with Madame Helga had bonded the group closely and made them believe that they were fated to stick together, even if they had differences of opinion. But it bothered Leila that she couldn't dismiss what Sandra was doing on the stage as easily as Ridley or Carter or Theo.

Still, Leila knew there was something powerful about seeing Madame Esmeralda do her thing. She was as wonderful at predictions as Leila was at escape artistry. The proof was in the faces of the audience as they watched and listened in awe. And despite the reservations Leila was feeling, she couldn't wait to talk to her dad's old friend after the show and learn how all of it worked.

On the stage, only the conservative-looking couple was left standing with the psychic. Madame Esmeralda grew quiet and still and serious. "A moment, audience...I am trying to speak with the other side...." She walked toward the red curtain at the rear of the stage and tilted her head as if listening to the voice of another spirit. She whispered something under her breath.

From the front row, Leila concentrated on the psychic's lips. She could have sworn Sandra said something like "*I won't do it.*"

Leila remembered hearing Sandra argue with herself in the resort's lounge the other day. Were spirits attacking her? Leila was just starting to worry that the show was about to go off the rails when, with no warning, Madame Esmeralda removed the turban from her head and threw it off stage. Two messy braids had been hidden underneath, and they fell to her shoulders.

She wasn't Madame Esmeralda anymore. She'd transformed into Sandra again. Her star-shaped earrings swung furiously as she stared up into the spotlight, holding her fingertips to her temples.

"I'm sorry," she said weakly to the couple. Everyone in the audience leaned forward in rapt attention. "There's something I *must* tell you, as much as it might pain me, and others...." The couple cringed, as if Sandra might suddenly leap at them. "You came here tonight looking for answers, did you not?"

The man in the brown suit cleared his throat and wrapped his arm around his wife, in the brown dress. She nodded to Sandra, who continued, "Then you won't be surprised to learn...your answers are *here* in this very room right now."

The woman's mouth dropped open, and she wiped at a tear that was creeping from the corner of her eye.

"This is about your daughter, is it not?" Sandra asked.

"It is," said the man. "We lost our girl a long, long time ago."

"We were so young then," said the woman. "We were broke and didn't have the means to provide her a good life. Before she was born, we agreed to give her up, but then we saw her smile...." She glanced at the man, as if asking for permission to continue. He nodded. "We wanted desperately to keep her; we wanted to give her everything, treat her like a little princess, but it wasn't realistic. With the help of a trusted friend, we relinquished custody....But not a day has passed that we haven't thought about her. Every day since, we have hoped that she is well. But now...now we want her back."

"We've *always* wanted her back," said the man. "We've worked hard to make something of ourselves, so that we could give her the life she deserves...."

Whispering rose up from the audience. People seemed to be wondering if this was actually part of the show. It felt so different from what had come before.

Sandra stared at the two intensely, as if she were ransacking their memories. She brought her index finger up to the center of her forehead. Closing her eyes, she asked, "Your names...please tell me."

The woman spoke haltingly, glancing at her partner every few words. "Pammy and Bob Varalika. We... we drove an hour and a half just to see you, Madame Esmeralda."

"Do you know where our girl is?" asked the man, a desperate tinge to his voice.

"I—I believe that I do," Sandra stammered nervously. "As a matter of fact...your daughter is...She is..." It was as if Sandra couldn't get the words out. "She's right here tonight."

"*Here?*" the couple echoed in disbelief.

When Sandra looked toward the Magic Misfits, Leila knew that she was searching for eye contact.

"Was your daughter's name *Leila*?" Sandra asked without looking away.

Leila felt as though the entire room had dropped out from underneath her. She sensed a vague pulling as Ridley grasped her wrist.

The Varalikas had both turned pale. The woman, Pammy, looked faint, and the man, Bob, clutched his wife's shoulders as if to hold her up. "That's correct," said Bob. "Just like the girl who performed before you. The escape artist. But you don't mean...She couldn't be..." He followed Sandra's gaze to the front row. By now, loud murmurs filled the room as the crowd's agitation grew and grew.

Wearing a sad look, Sandra held out her hand, her fingers trembling. "My dear Leila," she whispered. "Come up and meet your birth parents."

TWENTY-TWO

Leila couldn't do it alone.

Carter and Theo had to help her up the steps at the side of the stage as the audience clapped awkwardly. They seemed as confused as she was.

Leila noticed her poppa pushing through the crowd, heading toward the stage. He wore a look of shock and hurt that Leila had never seen on him before. She knew that there was no meal he could cook up that would soothe his soul tonight.

"Audience, it's been a pleasure to share my gifts with you this evening," Sandra said to the crowd, "but for now, we must offer privacy to this reunited family. May all of you take care."

With that, the heavy velvet curtain landed at the front of the stage with a resounding *whump*, blocking the audience's view. The scattered applause died out and was replaced by the white noise of loud conversation. A thousand voices talking at once. Leila was struck suddenly with the thought that this news would fly around town quicker than she could pick a lock.

The couple stood next to Sandra, who was holding out her arms to Leila. Leaving Carter and Theo behind, Leila fell into the embrace. Sandra squeezed her tightly. "It's a miracle," Sandra said quietly. "Your parents...your *real* parents have finally found you." Leila couldn't answer. She knew who her parents were. Neither of them was on this stage. She didn't have to be psychic to comprehend that. Carter and Theo stood back near the stairs, giving the group some space, but Leila wished they'd come closer. A nameless fear was making her feel woozy.

With the curtain closed, they had at least a little privacy. The stagehands stood in the wings, pretending to not listen.

Sandra made introductions. The Varalikas stared

at Leila as if she were a unicorn. Their eyes were wide and watery, their mouths slack with astonishment. Leila found it nearly impossible to look at them. Long ago, she'd promised herself to stop wondering where she'd come from. It was a shock to have the question whoosh back into her brain.

The adults were talking to her—asking her things— but she couldn't hear any of it. The only noise backstage was her heartbeat pounding at her eardrums. She didn't know what to think or what to do. She felt as though a closet door were closing on her, as though shoelaces were biting into her skin as the girls at Mother Margaret's Home tied her wrists before leaving her alone to figure out how to undo the knots. Instinct told her to run away. To leave everyone behind and protect herself. Leila had long ago learned to escape, but it was not often she wished to vanish as well.

Suddenly, a reassuring voice called out from behind her. "Leila!" Her poppa was galumphing across the stage, his heavy footsteps shaking the floor. Then his warm arms were around her as he hugged her close. After, he stepped in front of her, as if to protect her from the strangers. "Who are you people?" he asked.

"I'm a professor," Mrs. Varalika answered.

"I'm a banker," said Mr. Varalika. They turned back to Leila. "And this is—we hope it is—our daughter. May we ask: Is your birthday on February twelfth?"

"You don't have to answer them, Leila," Poppa said, turning to her. He looked her in the eyes. "If you want to, you can, but you don't have to. Tell me what you want, and I'll support you." He squeezed her hand, reassuringly.

Finally, after a long time, she nodded to the couple. "Yes, that's my birthday. At least according to the note pinned to the basket that Mother Margaret found me in." The couple's eyes grew glassy and wet.

"Tell me," said Mrs. Varalika. "Do you still have the pair of freckles that look like owl eyes on the back of your ankle?" Leila's skin prickled. She lifted the cuff of her pants to show the woman that she was right. "It *is* her!" Mrs. Varalika whispered to her husband. "Our daughter! I can't believe this!"

"Neither do I," Poppa growled. He stared daggers at Sandra and the couple. "I'm not trying to be rude, but you must understand—this is a lot to take in. This is *my* daughter, and—"

Sandra stared at the floor. The Varalikas' expressions were of worry and confusion. Mr. Varalika whispered, "We understand. This is an impossible situation. But we'd love to just sit and talk with Leila for a while. Would that be all right?"

"I—I honestly don't know," the Other Mr. Vernon said. He looked at Leila, who hadn't shed a tear but was filled to brimming on the inside. She felt as if she might burst. Poppa could see her turmoil. And he answered the Varalikas: "Perhaps another time. Right now, I need to get my daughter home. If you'll excuse us."

Poppa took her hand and led her back to the stairs at the side of the stage. She turned to glance at the couple one last time. The woman raised a mournful hand as if to say good-bye, and a phantom pain bloomed in Leila's chest, right underneath the key.

The Misfits followed their friend and her father down the hall and into his work kitchen. Then Leila's poppa phoned her other dad to explain what had happened. Poppa's voice hitched, and he put his hand over the receiver, covering his mouth at the same time to mask the conversation. The two Mr. Vernons spoke on the phone while the kids sat around one of the island counters in the center of the resort kitchen.

"Leila," Ridley started, hugging her friend. "What was that all about? Was it part of the act?"

Leila was too stunned to respond.

"Of course it was," said Izzy.

"Every act needs a little *drama*," Olly added. "Or in this case, *a lot!*"

Izzy punched her brother in the arm. "Let's practice the quiet game, Mr. Insensitive."

Carter took hold of Leila's limp hand while Theo squeezed her shoulder, as if either of those actions might shock her into responding.

Ridley rubbed Leila's arm. "You're gonna be okay."

"But that's the question," Leila said with a groan. *"Am I?"*

The others looked at her as if she'd just said a swear. But she was too upset and confused to apologize. Carter and Theo winced. Even Olly and Izzy, who almost always wore smiles, looked worried.

"*We're* here for you," said Ridley.

Leila blinked. "I just hope I can still be *here* with you."

"Of course," said Theo. "Where else would you be?"

"With *them*." Leila nodded in the direction of the auditorium, as if that was where the Varalikas lived now.

"But they can't do that," said Carter. "The Vernons adopted you. *We're* your family."

"I know. But do the Varalikas know that?"

"Does Sandra?" asked Ridley.

"Of course she does," said Leila. "She's one of my dad's oldest friends. I'm sure that what happened on the stage hurt her as much as it did the rest of us. It was almost as if she didn't want to share the revelation. But she knew she had to tell the truth."

Ridley stared at her for a moment. "I'm sure you're right." But Ridley didn't look at all sure about any of it.

✷ ✷ ✷

Leila returned with Carter and her poppa to the apartment above the magic shop. Her dad greeted her with the tightest hug he'd ever given her. "Oh, sweetheart..."

Leila felt her frame shaking. For a moment, she wasn't sure which of them was crying before she realized they both were. She let it out. All the fear. All the anger. It poured down her cheeks and soaked his jacket. Leila allowed herself to settle into the rhythm of his breathing, and soon, they landed together after her dizzying flight of worry. Finally, he asked, "Are you okay?"

Her instinct was to smile and brush away the tears, but she didn't wish to lie to him. "I'm happy to be home," she answered.

The phone rang. No one moved. None of them wanted the interruption. But when it went on and on, the jangling, clanging noise began to sound like an alarm. Mr. Vernon answered it. "What is it?" he asked. Almost immediately, his face turned bright red. "Oh, they have, have they? Tomorrow morning? No, that's not going to be good for us....Fine. If it must be done, I suppose we don't have a choice. We'll be there."

"What's wrong?" asked the Other Mr. Vernon. "Who was that?"

Mr. Vernon glanced at Leila and Carter with a look of doubt, as if he thought that maybe they shouldn't hear what he had to say. But then he just let it all out. "That couple, the Varalikas, booked a room at the resort and contacted a local lawyer. That was him. He's demanding we meet with them—all of us, including Leila and Carter—tomorrow morning at his office."

"Why?" Leila asked. "Are they going to try to take me away from you?"

Her fathers couldn't hide the worried look that passed between them. "Of course not," said Mr. Vernon. "They only want to *talk* to us. That's all."

✴ ✴ ✴

In the dead of night, Leila was lying in bed, staring at the ceiling like she'd done earlier that week. She was trying to not cry. She clasped her special key in her fist so tightly that she wondered if it might unlock something inside her, a secret she'd secured for forgotten reasons. It felt like the night of the circus monkey's arrival had been a hundred years ago. Was the little creature still out there? Maybe it was watching her right now, she thought.

On this night, Leila was not visited by the ghosts of things past. No Mother Margaret's Home for Children. No dark closets. No shoes tied together by naughty housemates. Now Leila worried about the phantom presence of an uncertain future. A future in which she might have to leave this place and the people she loved, all to follow a pair of strangers along a mist-enshrouded and possibly perilous trail.

There came a knocking at the wall—taps and scratching that created a peculiar but meaningful pattern. Carter was awake, sending her a message. Morse code.

•••• • •—• • / ••—• ——— •—• /
—•—— ——— ••—

She worked out the letters from the dots and dashes, thankful for the distraction. When she figured it out, she smiled. She thought for a while, then knocked her knuckles and dragged her fingertips against the wallpaper in reply.

—— • / — ——— ——— /
•— •—•• •—— •— —•—— •••

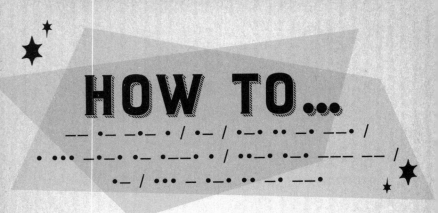

HOW TO...

`__ __ / ._ _._ . / ._ / ._.. .. _. __. / `
`. ... _._. ._ ._ ._.. . / ..._ ._ ___ __ / `
`._ / ... _ _._ .. _. __.`

My apologies! I was so caught up in the Morse code at the end of the previous chapter, I kept right on going. If you don't already know Morse code, I suggest checking the back of this book....

Anywho...Another night, another magic lesson. Are you up for it? Good. Let's learn one of Leila's escape tricks! Here goes!

WHAT YOU'LL NEED:

First, you'll need to be dressed in a long-sleeve shirt.

A length of string or thin rope (a spare shoelace will do in a pinch)

A piece of paper

A pair of scissors (Remember what I said about grown-ups and sharp objects? They go together like toast and jam. In other words, keep one around for safety.)

A dark handkerchief or small towel

A volunteer from the audience

TO PREPARE:

You will need to cut out two identical rings from the paper. They should be big enough to fit the string through their centers—a few inches wide at most. In fact, you might as well cut out several more rings while you're at it so that you can use them to *practice, practice, practice*. However, for the trick itself, you'll only need *two*.

SECRET MAGIC MOVE:

Before your audience arrives, hide one of the paper rings inside your sleeve.

STEPS:

1. Choose a volunteer from your audience.

2. Slip the second paper ring onto the string, then hand the ends of the string to your volunteer. Ask them to hold on tightly and then have them raise the string loosely for all to see.

3. Explain that you plan on removing the ring from the string without damaging the ring, the string, the handkerchief, or your volunteer's fingers. . . all in fewer than ten seconds.

10... 9... 8...

4. Cover the string (and the ring) with the handkerchief and begin your countdown. TEN, NINE, EIGHT, and so forth. Place your hands beneath the cloth.

SECRET MAGIC MOVE:

Carefully tear the paper ring off the string and slip it inside the cuff of your empty sleeve. Then remove the hidden ring from your other sleeve.

5. As you count down to ONE, remove your hand holding the *intact* paper ring from underneath the cloth. *Huh—what?*

...1!

6. Using your other hand, pull away the handkerchief from the string, showing the audience that the string is whole and that the volunteer never let go. *Huzzah!*

7. Take a bow!

TWENTY-
THREE

The morning was bright and the sky was clear. By the time Leila, Carter, and the two Mr. Vernons made it to the lawyer's address, the sun was well on its way to wilting the lush valley and warming the rivers that snaked through the surrounding hills.

The brick building was two stories tall. Empty lots bordered the property on each side, and beyond those were thick patches of brush and brambles. A train horn blew in the distance, and a warm wind rocked the trees all around. The lawyer's name on the door appeared to be freshly painted, causing Mr. Vernon to raise an eyebrow.

The Other Mr. Vernon pulled open the door. At the far end of a long space, there was a big desk and several chairs arranged in a half circle. The two on the left were occupied by Mr. and Mrs. Varalika. The couple stood, practically trembling, as the Vernons approached with the kids.

Behind the desk sat a tall man in a stiff gray suit. His blond hair was brushed straight back, and his long nose reminded Leila of the beak of an eagle or some other bird of prey. "You must be the Vernons." The tall man rose to his feet and held out his hand, but only Mr. Vernon took it, and he did so reluctantly.

"I am Sammy Falsk, Esquire," the lawyer said. He turned his withering gaze toward Leila, and when he smiled, she shuddered. His teeth were as yellow as canary birds in a coal mine. "This young lady must be Leila. The Varalikas have filled me in on your plight. Please sit."

There was a sound back by the front door. Leila turned and saw a second desk, where another man was working—an unusually short man with a thick black mustache and a black bowler hat—typing away at an

ancient typewriter. He looked like he might be a partner or colleague of Mr. Falsk's. He paid her no attention.

The Other Mr. Vernon eased himself into one of
the stiff chairs, glancing suspiciously at the mostly
empty space. "Looks like you're still moving in," he
muttered.

"Yes, yes, new to town, lovely place," Sammy Falsk,
Esquire, answered.

As Leila sat, she searched for herself in the faces
of the Varalikas, trying to pick out features she might
have seen in her own mirror. The woman's nostrils

looked sort of familiar. And the man's earlobes were high and tight, like her own. But that was about it: a birth mother's nostrils and a birth father's earlobes. Not all children resemble their parents exactly, but Leila's genetic connection with the Varalikas did not appear to be strong. This was no relief.

She'd managed to make it through her entire performance without freezing with stage fright, but she feared that if anyone were to ask her a question now, her lips would seize up, and she'd look like she didn't know how to speak. It felt like a trap from which she would not escape. Carter caught her eye, and he winked. That helped a little bit. *Thank goodness for him*, she thought.

Sammy Falsk, Esquire, sat at the big desk and motioned for everyone else to sit too. He launched immediately into a grand spiel. "I have been an expert in family law for as long as I can remember, which, let me tell you, is a very long time. My first case involved a couple who was trying to regain custody of their child after both of them had gone missing during an expedition to..." His voice droned on and on.

All that Leila could think about was what she would do if she were forced to go live with these people who she didn't even know. How different would a professor and banker's home be from living over an actual magic shop?

"...after which," continued the lawyer, "I took a lovely vacation to Madrid with my third wife, whose full name was Francesca Domingue De Louisa Maria Benedictine Marzipan, who grew up in the south of..."

Leila tried to follow his story, but it was so nonsensical that her mind kept drifting and her eyes scanned the sad little office space. She noticed the lawyer near the front door was humming a tune under his breath. Leila thought it was a really odd thing to do during a serious legal discussion. The dust in the room was thick; the morning light filtering through the newspapered windows was a drowsy amber. Her fathers listened politely but wore stern expressions, their brows low, their mouths pinched, their hands folded in their laps. The Varalikas' smiles did not leave their faces.

And the lawyer played on: "Which brings me back to my original point. You just cannot trust a domesticated house cat—"

Mr. Vernon interrupted, "I'm sorry to stop you here, but would you mind getting to the business at hand?"

Sammy Falsk, Esquire, leaned forward. "Business? Yes. Let's get to it." He flipped through some papers in a manila file folder on the desk. "I have here a birth certificate with all the names and dates accounted for. Pammy, Bob, Leila. The Varalikas. All official."

The man near the front door continued to hum. Leila recognized the old folk ballad "Oh My Darling, Clementine." The sound of it was like fingernails running up Leila's spine.

Mr. Vernon held out his hand. "I'd like to take a closer look, if you please." But when Sammy Falsk, Esquire, placed the document onto Vernon's palm, a dark spot appeared in the center and spread quickly outward until the page was almost completely black. Leila recalled her father once performing a trick like this at the magic shop using a palmed inkpad. Mrs. Varalika shrieked.

"Oh my," said Mr. Vernon with a shrug. "So sorry. My mistake. I do hope you have another copy."

"As it so happens," said the lawyer, his face red as he pulled another sheet of paper from the folder, "I do. I must insist we be more careful with this one, however. You may look but may *not* touch."

Leila couldn't bring herself to get any closer to it. As if sensing her discomfort, Carter took her hand, and she sighed. The Other Mr. Vernon stood up and bent over the desk, peering at the birth certificate. His cheeks went slack. "It looks real enough."

Mr. Vernon poked him in the back. "A magician knows that *real enough* doesn't mean *authentic*, my dear."

The hum continued: "*Oh my darling, oh my darling...*" Leila noticed that Carter seemed to be irked by the humming as well.

"What exactly is your purpose in bringing us here today?" Mr. Vernon asked the Varalikas.

"Isn't it obvious?" Pammy responded. "We need to work out a way to bring our baby home with us."

Leila felt the blood drain out of her face. The room tilted, and she grasped one side of the chair to stop from toppling over. The Other Mr. Vernon held her forearm tightly, while Carter continued to grip her hand.

"Such an interesting request," said Mr. Vernon with a grin.

Why does he look happy? Leila thought. No. Not happy. There was something in his eyes that was...what? Devious? Assured? Leila wondered if there was a way to tap into whatever he was feeling. It would certainly feel better than the helplessness that was binding her like ropes around her torso.

"We understand that this process will not be easy," the lawyer continued. "But what I hope to begin this very day is some sort of negotiation to allow Leila to spend some time with the Varalikas. To get to know them. Slowly. Over time. We certainly wouldn't ask to make any abrupt changes."

"Of course not. *Abrupt* changes are the worst sort of changes to make." Mr. Vernon nodded emphatically. "Like showing up in town after a lifetime and asking a girl to change her entire world."

"Dante, please," the Other Mr. Vernon said quietly. Then he turned to Leila. "This decision isn't up to me or your father. This is up to you. And we'll support you no matter what you decide. Please, tell us: Is this something that *you'd* like to do, Leila?"

"I—I don't..." Leila was still waiting for an answer to come to her, telling her what to feel. Right now, it was all anxiety and anger and confusion and thunder and lightning and gale-force winds and flying cows and maybe a little bit of Dorothy singing sweetly about places beyond rainbows, which was exactly where Leila wanted to be at the moment. Her skin flushed with heat and pain. She clutched at the key beneath her shirt, and it brought her back to earth.

Carter started squeezing her hand in an odd way. She glanced at him, but he purposefully kept his eyes focused on the humming lawyer. Within seconds, Leila recognized what Carter was doing: making a pattern, sending her a Morse code message.

$$\bullet\bullet\bullet \ {-}{-}{-} \ \bullet\bullet\bullet \ / \ \bullet\bullet\bullet \ {-}{-}{-} \ \bullet\bullet\bullet \ / \ \bullet\bullet\bullet \ {-}{-}{-} \ \bullet\bullet\bullet$$

SOS. SOS. SOS. The universal sign for distress. She squeezed back, saying:

$$\bullet{-}{-} \ \bullet\bullet\bullet\bullet \ \bullet{-} \ {-} \ / \ \bullet\bullet \ \bullet\bullet\bullet \ /$$
$$\bullet{-}{-} \ \bullet{-}\bullet \ {-}{-}{-} \ {-}\bullet \ {-}{-}\bullet$$

The lawyers didn't seem to notice them communicating in this way. Falsk blathered on about "next steps" and about the law being on *his* side.

In the meantime, Carter squeezed more Morse code. Leila slowly deciphered it.

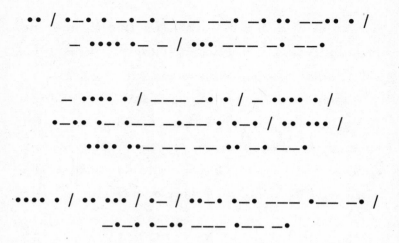

Leila couldn't help leaping to her feet in shock.

Everyone turned to look at her. "Leila?" asked Mr. Vernon. "What is it?" But Leila couldn't answer. There was too much happening in her head.

No, she thought. *It can't be. What on earth would a member of Bosso's old crew be doing here in...* Then it came to her. *Everything about these people...Mr. and Mrs. Varalika. What if... what if they* weren't *really her parents?*

"What do you know about keys?" she managed to squeak out.

Mrs. Varalika appeared to be confused. "Keys?"

Actually, both Mr. Vernons looked confused too. Only Carter gave her a knowing glance.

The small man near the door stopped humming. He peered over, a sharp glint in his expression.

"Yes. *Keys*. Or rather...one key in particular."

Something registered in the Varalikas' eyes. "We don't know much," Mrs. Varalika answered stiffly. "They unlock things. Doors and such?"

That was all she needed. Leila was certain. The mention of her key should have meant the world to them! These people were *not* the ones who had left her on the steps of Mother Margaret's Home for Children. There was no way she'd let them take her anywhere. Then she had a creepier thought: *If they're not my birth parents, then what are they doing here? Why would they lie?*

Carter's message blinked back into her brain. *Frown clown.* What if it wasn't just one member of Bosso's old crew who was in town? What if it was *all* of them?

"Never mind," she said, her throat constricting. "I was...confused. Sorry." As soon as she took her seat, she began tapping on the arm of her chair. Vernon took notice.

••—• •—• ——— •—— —• /

—•—• •—•• ——— •—— —•

Mr. Vernon nodded that he understood his daughter. "Well, this all sounds splendid! What a wonderful meeting. You have our phone number, so please, call us later. I am sure we'll be able to work it all out. But for now, our family must be going."

"Not yet, please," said the fake lawyer. "We still have so much to go over."

"Another time!" Mr. Vernon said. He nodded to the Other Mr. Vernon. Without hesitation, each Mr. Vernon took one of the kids by the hand and marched them toward the exit across the long room. But the Varalikas rushed past them to block the door. The man who'd been humming got up and joined them. The three were now standing in the way, none of them smiling.

Sammy Falsk, Esquire, also joined his partners in front of the exit. All three men stuck their hands into their jacket pockets and pulled out long black billy clubs that looked thick enough to knock a person unconscious. Mr. Varalika, wearing a frown, said, "You and your brats aren't going anywhere."

TWENTY-FOUR

"They're the frown clowns from Bosso's circus!" Carter cried out. "I recognized the humming!"

"And those aren't my real parents," Leila added, nodding to the Varalikas. "They didn't know about my key." The Vernons didn't understand, but they trusted their daughter. They stepped between their children and the frown clowns.

The four villains glanced at one another and smirked.

"Aren't you kids just the *smartest*?" the small man

sneered, pulling his black mustache off his top lip and tossing it aside.

"Quiet, Tommy," said Mr. Varalika. "You don't want to give 'em big heads." Grabbing his toupee from his bald scalp, he added, "Good lord, this thing is itchy."

"Step aside," said the Other Mr. Vernon, his fists squeezed tightly. "We don't want anyone to get hurt here."

"Our boss would kill us if we were to let you go so soon," said Mrs. Varalika, removing a smaller club from her purse before stepping forward and forcing the group back into the depths of the office.

"Your boss?" Carter asked. "You mean Bosso escaped from jail?!"

"Bosso?" asked Falsk with a laugh. "That old clown was never in charge of anything or anyone. No, I don't believe you've yet met our *true* leader."

"Your true leader?" Leila repeated, her usual confidence suddenly flooding back into her body. Now that she knew these folks were frauds, it was easier to talk back to them. "Who might that be?"

The four former frown clowns only chuckled.

Mr. Vernon whipped his hand up over his head and then brought it down quickly. All of a sudden, smoke was rising from the floor, swirling around the family, hiding them from the villains. "Quick! Follow me!" But before Leila could move, she felt herself being yanked backward.

She yelped, calling through the smoke, "Dad! Poppa! Help!"

The fake lawyer's voice boomed out as he held Leila's arms behind her back. "If you want to keep the girl safe, you'll stop where you are!"

As the smoke dissipated, Mr. Vernon raised his hands in surrender. The Varalikas flanked them. The fake lawyer nodded toward the doorway at the back of the room. "Move it. All of you. Into the basement. And no funny business."

A flight of stairs led down into shadow. Falsk shoved them all forward. Leila was the last through, and she thought almost fondly of the closet at Mother Margaret's Home. Being locked in a closet by bullies was far better than being mishandled by sinister frown clowns. Leila nearly stumbled down the steps, but her fathers caught her. From the top of the stairs, the fake lawyer called to them, "We would have tied you up, but we saw what Leila can do to a knot. Let's see her escape a basement, though."

The four villains waved, then shut the door. Moments later, the door shuddered as they hammered nails into the frame. Shadows filled Leila's vision at the bottom of the steps. Her fathers were immediately at her side, kneeling and hugging her in the darkness. Mr. Vernon asked, "Are you okay, dear? Did they hurt you?"

"I'm fine," Leila whispered. "What about all of you?"

"Don't worry about us," said the Other Mr. Vernon. "I'm sorry that we agreed to bring you two out here. What a horrible mistake." The group huddled together. Leila's eyes were beginning to adjust when Carter pulled the trusty flashlight out of his satchel and flicked it on.

"*Oh my darling, Clementine,*" whispered Carter, waving the light around the space, but the beam illuminated nothing. The walls were too far away. "All those weeks ago, when Bosso's security first brought me into his circus trailer, one of those frown clowns was singing that song. It took me a while to make the connection."

"Nice work with the Morse code, you two," said Mr. Vernon. "There are reasons I keep so many different kinds of books in the magic shop. And most of those reasons aren't because I mean to sell them."

"You can thank Ridley," said Leila, "if we ever manage to escape."

Her dad raised his eyebrow. "What do you mean, *if*? You are Leila Vernon. You can escape anything!"

Footsteps clunked overhead. The former clowns were walking around. "What are they up to?" Carter asked. "Are they going to hurt us?"

The Other Mr. Vernon shushed him. "Listen."

A muffled voice said something like "...meet the others at the shop, gotta find that book..." Then steps moved toward the front. There was a squeaking sound and a door slamming. Afterward, an eerie silence echoed through the old office.

Both Mr. Vernons ran to the top of the stairs and pushed against the door. "No luck. They nailed it shut," said the Other Mr. Vernon.

Leila's fathers came back down the stairs. "Would you mind if I borrowed the light for a moment?" Vernon asked. He took Carter's flashlight and searched the room. "No windows, no shovels, no hammers or crowbars to punch through the door. A shame I don't have a large ax up my sleeve."

Just then, the flashlight beam alighted on an empty bookshelf. Vernon went to examine it, then pushed it aside. Behind it, a rusted door was embedded into the building's stone foundation.

Leila and Carter gasped.

The Other Mr. Vernon peered into the darkness. "What's wrong? What do you see?"

Carter swallowed nervously. "The door looks like one we discovered in the basement of the Grand Oak's lodge two days ago. The symbol over the keyhole—"

Leila flinched, then quickly interrupted him. "The map we found at the resort hinted that there are bootlegging tunnels under the town." She blinked at Vernon. "But then, you probably knew that already. Since it was *your* map."

"My map?"

"The one in the metal box buried under the stone floor of the lodge's abandoned wing," said Carter.

Leila added, "The one that was decoded by a cipher coin that magically appeared in our magic shop?"

A brief, impressed smile crossed Mr. Vernon's face. "But that wasn't *my* map."

"*The Emerald Ring's map*, then," said Carter. "We thought that Leila's key would fit the lock, but it didn't."

Leila felt like a clamp was suddenly crushing her temples. She wanted to squeeze Carter's wrist to tell him to shut his mouth, but it was already too late. Her fathers scrunched up their foreheads, confused. "Key?" asked Mr. Vernon. "What key?"

Carter clapped his hand over his mouth and glanced at Leila in horror. He knew he'd unleashed her secret.

"Is this what you were talking about upstairs, honey?" asked the Other Mr. Vernon. "When you wanted to know if those frauds knew anything about—"

Leila sighed and nodded. She felt exhausted from keeping this secret. It was way past time to let her parents in on what she'd kept to herself for so long—proof of her past, proof that her birth parents had thought enough of her to leave a memento, a hint of where she'd come from, of who she really was, of the person she was capable of becoming.

Tugging at the string around her neck, she finally showed the key to her fathers. Mr. Vernon couldn't control his surprise. His jaw swiveled open like a trapdoor in a stage.

Words came from her mouth, sounding to her like she was speaking from inside a dream. "Dad, Poppa... long before I met you, when someone left me on the steps of Mother Margaret's Home, they placed this key in my bassinet. I've cherished it ever since. I never told you about it because...well, I didn't want you to think that I needed to be chained to my old life. I love you both very much. But I couldn't let this token go. I feel like sometimes...it helps keep me safe."

The men clasped hands, then hugged Leila close again. They nearly squeezed tears out of her.

"The Emerald Ring used that old skeleton key to access the tunnels and unlock other doors around Mineral Wells," said Mr. Vernon. "We kept it in a hiding place at the magic shop so that we could all use it whenever we wanted."

Something about this statement struck a chime in Leila's head. "Does that mean...someone in the Emerald Ring is one of my biological parents?"

Mr. Vernon stared at her for a few seconds, gears turning, as if he was trying to think of a response. "I don't know about that, Leila," he said finally, sincerely. For now, Leila let the question go. "Let's see if the old thing still works." Mr. Vernon led the group toward the rusted door.

"We tried the key in a door at the Grand Oak the other day," said Carter. "No luck."

Leila stuck the key into the lock, and just as she expected, it did not turn.

"Ah yes," said Mr. Vernon. "But this is a special lock. And you are holding a special key."

Leila felt her entire body buzz, as if her dad were about to share the secret of one of his most enigmatic tricks. She said, "But it doesn't work."

"A key works only if you know how to use it," Mr. Vernon said. "And a *magician's key* might be misleading."

"Misdirection," Leila whispered.

She stared at the key, particularly the end with the ornamental club-suit decoration. Perhaps it wasn't ornamental at all. She removed the string, then inserted the key—in reverse—into the keyhole. This time when she turned her wrist, the old rusted door let out a loud metallic *click*—satisfying in every way—and the large door swung open.

TWENTY-FIVE

The Vernon family hurried through the darkness. Mr.
Vernon held the flashlight, directing the glow ahead of
them. Carter clutched the map of the tunnels, trying
to discern exactly where they were.

The tunnel was several feet wide and almost six feet
tall. Some parts of it looked as though they'd been
carved out by ancient underground streams; the walls
were smooth stone with scalloped edges near the top.
Other parts appeared to have been hacked directly
through the bedrock by bootlegger pickaxes. In some
sections, wooden joists arced overhead, providing

support against the weight of the earth. In others, the group had to step over piles of stone that had rained recklessly down from the ceiling over the years, weakening the structure. Leila stumbled over a post lying flat across the floor. There were iron rails running through the tunnel, wooden slats connecting them like train tracks.

"Where did the Emerald Ring get the skeleton key, Dad?" Leila asked, her voice echoing out into the darkness.

"Oh, didn't I say?" Mr. Vernon asked. But then he was quiet.

"No," Leila answered. "You didn't *say*, Dad. You never do."

"My apologies," he replied quietly. The Other Mr. Vernon rubbed his back. "The truth is, I am sort of ashamed about where my old club got that skeleton key."

"Ashamed?" asked Carter. "Why?"

Mr. Vernon blurted out, "We stole it from Sandra's father." His statement echoed all around them.

Slowly, it settled in Leila's mind, ripples of meaning meandering through her body. Questions flooded her brain. All this time, she'd thought that what she wanted most was answers. Now she was terrified of finally learning them, more terrified than she was of the tunnel collapsing.

Still, she asked him, "Why...why did Sandra's father have the key in the first place?"

"He was Mineral Wells's locksmith," Mr. Vernon answered simply. "He crafted a skeleton key specially for the former mayor of Mineral Wells. Mr. Santos was also the man who built the metal doors that sealed up the bootlegging tunnels beneath the town. The mayor was worried about people crawling around down here and the passages collapsing, so he hired Santos to forge an impossibly strong lock that would keep out trespassers."

"Trespassers like the Emerald Ring?" Carter asked.

"Exactly!"

Leila and Carter glanced at each other, confused. They moved carefully onward, following Mr. Vernon toward what they hoped was the center of Mineral Wells and another rusted door that Leila's key might unlock.

"Unfortunately, what the mayor feared came to pass," Mr. Vernon went on. "But the only victim was the man trying to protect the town. Sandra's father died down here when one of the tunnels crumpled. She was devastated."

"That's terrible!" said Carter.

Leila felt her face grow warm. "Poor thing."

Mr. Vernon nodded. "Sandra was so distraught that she hid the map and the key from the rest of us in the Emerald Ring, so that no one would ever get hurt in the tunnels again. You kids were clever enough to solve her riddle and uncover her long-buried secret."

"But," Carter said, his brow furrowed, "none of that answers how *Leila* ended up with the key in the first place."

Mr. Vernon glanced at his husband.

"It's probably best to keep our voices down," said the Other Mr. Vernon quickly. "If those clowns circle back to the law office and figure out that we've left the basement, we might give away our location." Mr. Vernon nodded again, then pointed toward a shadowy opening in the tunnel wall.

The Other Mr. Vernon went first—his shoulders hunched so he wouldn't bump his head on the low ceiling—listening for any hint of danger.

As Leila followed Carter, she held her breath. She concentrated on maneuvering through the dark, even though she was unsure what might happen when they made it back to the light. Had Sandra Santos's father been the *only* person who had perished down here? Leila's mind whirled. What if they came across a skeleton—a real one this time? What if it started dancing like the one in the basement of the resort? And what about the spirits that Sandra had invited into the auditorium the previous night? What if they were still hanging around in Mineral Wells?

Pebbles fell from a crack in the ceiling, and everyone froze, panicked that their next move might set off a perilous chain reaction. After a tense few moments, the pebbles stopped falling, and the group continued on carefully past the crack.

When they came to a fork in the tunnel, Mr. Vernon pointed down a dark path. "This way. I think."

"You think?" asked the Other Mr. Vernon.

Carter held the bootlegging map in front of the flashlight beam. "He's right. We're moving in the right direction."

"Thank you, my boy."

"Thanks to the bootleggers," Carter added, "and that the magic shop used to be a jazz club."

On and on they walked. Ahead, Leila's poppa paused. "Does any of this look familiar?"

"It all looks the same, if that's what you mean," said her dad. "It's a bit of a labyrinth, isn't it?" This was not reassuring. Mr. Vernon seemed to realize that Leila's face was a mask of worry. "Then again, life is but a labyrinth that we must navigate blindfolded. Is it not?"

"A little on the nose," her poppa responded. "But fair enough."

Leila shushed them, frustrated that she suddenly felt like the parent.

"There!" Carter shouted. Leila followed his gaze

and noticed that the flashlight's beam had landed on what looked like a set of stone steps. At the top was another rusted door. Hopefully, the way out.

Throwing caution to the shadows, Leila raced ahead, clutching her key in her fist. She felt around for the keyhole and then placed the butt end of the key inside. With a *click*, the latch released. When Leila pushed the door, it squealed and gave way.

TWENTY-SIX

Pushing past a dusty velvet curtain and into a shadowy room, Leila caught a whiff of something familiar—musty but comforting, bringing sweet and happy feelings to the surface. The flashlight beam revealed a folding table leaning against a stone wall. There were cardboard boxes stacked all around, labeled with black ink: X-RAY SPECS, TALKING SKULLS, LARGE IMP BOTTLES, RUBBER PENCILS. They were in the basement of the magic shop!

"We made it!" said Carter, wiping wet cobwebs from the tunnels off his shoulders. But before anyone could say anything else, a crash sounded from upstairs.

Another crash reverberated down. Mr. Vernon motioned for everyone to be quiet. He waved them all toward the stairs. They climbed, careful not to tread on the squeakiest steps.

At the top, the four barreled into the magic shop and saw someone duck behind the counter.

"Who goes there?" demanded Mr. Vernon, stepping forward and stretching out his arms as if to protect the rest of them.

A soft voice croaked, "Dante?"

"Sandra?" Leila said, rushing over. She found the woman crouching down beside the counter, wearing a deep purple housedress. In one hand, she clutched her large burgundy purse with the embroidered crystal ball on it. Sandra looked at Leila in shock, then stood up. "You startled me!" She glanced at the others. "Where did you all come from?"

Carter pointed toward the basement door.

Sandra's breath heaved. "I thought...I thought that maybe some spirits were after me." Her voice rose dramatically, and she held her hand to her forehead.

Leila glanced around the shop. It was in shambles. Books had been thrown from the shelves, drawers jarred open, magical items strewn every which way.

"What are you doing here, Sandra?" Mr. Vernon's voice was stern.

The Other Mr. Vernon stood beside him. "The door was locked. How did you get in?"

Sandra's cheeks flushed. "Oh, well, I came by to check on Leila, to see if everything was okay after last night. I found the door open and the store a mess. I thought you'd been robbed!" Her voice trembled. "I was just about to head upstairs when you all came up from the basement."

Mr. Vernon shook his head. "You *knew* we were meeting with that couple and the man who called himself their lawyer, didn't you?"

"I knew nothing about a meeting," Sandra said, looking confused. "How did they find a lawyer so quickly?"

"That's the thing," said the Other Mr. Vernon. "They *didn't.*"

Leila squinted at Sandra, trying to see beyond the woman's act. To Leila's surprise, her own voice came out cold, like an icy stone at the bottom of a frozen lake. "They weren't who they said they were....They were Bosso's frown clowns. Except they don't work for Bosso. They work for someone else. When we tried to leave, they locked us in the basement. We escaped through the old bootlegging tunnels and ended up back here at the shop."

Sandra shook her head in shock. "Thank goodness you're all right. Those people sound horrible!"

"There are many words I'd use to describe them," the Other Mr. Vernon growled. "*Horrible* would be the nicest."

Carter approached the counter and ran his fingers over several piles of marbleized ledgers sitting there. "These look just like the notebook that the monkey tried to take from Mr. Vernon's office. We usually keep them tucked neatly behind the counter. If someone broke in to rob the store, why would they pile them up here? Unless..." His eyes popped open wide as an idea came to him. "Unless the person who broke in was still looking for that same ledger, the one from Mr. Vernon's office."

Sandra stepped swiftly away from Carter, but not before he snatched another marbleized notebook from her crystal-ball purse and held it up. Sandra gasped, then looked at Leila, who was appalled. The group stared at Sandra in shocked silence.

After a few seconds, Sandra said softly, "I can explain."

A violent dizziness seemed to crush Leila's head, and she had to hold on to a bookshelf to keep from collapsing. *No...no...it can't be true....*Everything she'd admired about this woman fell away...*Please*, Leila thought. *Please don't let her say what I know she's going to say... that's she's one of the bad guys...*

"They weren't supposed to hurt you," Sandra went on. "*Under no circumstances*, I told them. I made them *promise* me."

Mr. Vernon clutched the Other Mr. Vernon's shoulder. His voice broke as he said, "Oh, Sandra... how could you?"

"I had to do it," she said. "You don't understand, Dante. Kalagan forced me to. You know how he works. He can make anyone do anything."

Leila was surprised to hear herself echo the name. "Kalagan?"

Sandra's eyes grew wide. "A mesmerist. He has powers...*terrible* powers."

"The only power Kalagan ever had was the power to manipulate," Mr. Vernon spat. "He was never the real deal."

"He's real enough," said Sandra. "It doesn't matter if you *believe* in him....He will always seek to destroy what he cannot control. And once he has control, you'll *believe* whatever he wants you to."

Carter asked, "Who is Kalagan?! What are you talking about?!"

Vernon retrieved the old sepia-toned photo of the Emerald Ring. There they all were—young and fresh and full of life and love for one another. Sandra was holding her crystal ball. Bobby Boscowitz was grinning slyly. A bespectacled boy sat with a doll on his lap. Behind him, Lyle Locke—Carter's father—was laughing as Dante Vernon looked on, lost in thought. And at the edge of the group, a figure in a cape and top hat stood in shadow, as if shrinking from the light, trying to hide away from the others.

Leila's mind wandered back to the abandoned wing of the Grand Oak, and she recalled the messages and symbols that had been written on the walls, and the poster, and the stones in the basement floor. All of it had been the work of these kids. Their group had been so close once. But now that was over. They'd broken apart, scattered to the wind. Bosso had turned into a big bully, and now Sandra...

Leila piped up. "At the lodge, we saw initials carved into the wall. *K* and *A*. Kalagan...and who else?"

Sandra breathed heavily. "My full name is Alessandra Santos. I can't tell you how many times I crossed out the graffiti in that room. But Kalagan just kept carving it again. He was obsessed with me." Her eyes were wild, desperate.

Mr. Vernon tapped at the photo, on the shadowy figure. "*This* is Kalagan." Leila was yanked out of her imagination and back into the magic shop. Vernon glanced at Sandra, pain in his eyes. "He's the reason that the Emerald Ring fell to pieces all those years ago. The fire at the hotel...the candle, and the trick we begged him not to do..."

Leila's heart jolted—so her dad *did* know about the accident in the abandoned wing after all. And it had been Kalagan's doing! Carter's eyes flicked toward her own, sending a secret message of understanding.

Mr. Vernon sighed. "What did he ask you to do, Sandra?"

Tears gathered the black mascara from Sandra's

eyelashes and made it streak down her face like smeared clown makeup. "It started with the monkey."

It was such a ridiculous sentence that if Leila weren't so queasy, she might have guffawed.

"I suspected as much." Mr. Vernon nodded knowingly. "Monkeys don't usually break into apartments in the middle of the night."

Sandra scoffed and then sniffed. "Monkeys don't usually follow the orders of lunatic carnival owners either. But somehow Bosso managed to train the creature to do his bidding. When Bosso was caught, some of his clowns escaped. But they never really were *his* crew. Ultimately, they've always answered to Kalagan. Their *true leader*. He had the clowns send the monkey to break into your office, to retrieve a book that you were writing in, but then the little turncoat refused to come back. So...who does Kalagan send to finish the monkey's task?"

"*That's* why you came back to Mineral Wells?" Carter asked, astonished. He tucked the notebook he'd taken from her tightly under his arm, then placed his hands atop the piles of ledgers on the counter. "To rob Mr. Vernon?"

Sandra hung her head, unable to answer the question. "That night at dinner, after I excused myself to the bathroom, I quietly scoured Dante's office for the book. No luck. I figured he might have moved it down to the shop. But then the monkey screeched, scaring me half to death. I was so flustered I fell. It's like the monkey wanted me to get caught."

Mr. Vernon bit his bottom lip. "I did suspect that something was up."

"I knew then that I had to leave Mineral Wells and never return." Sandra sniffed and then shuddered. "But Kalagan wouldn't allow it. He made certain that the manager of the Grand Oak offered me a show. And I believed that if Leila were to perform with me, your whole family would have been out of the shop long enough for the clowns to sneak in and find the book."

"You mean...you didn't *really* think I was talented?" Leila asked. It felt as if Sandra were plucking her petals, throwing them to the floor, and then crushing them beneath her heel.

"Your talent is unquestionable, honey. But it wasn't in the center of my mind." She shook her head and reached out to touch Leila's shoulder. Leila flinched, and Sandra seemed to think better of it. "This next part is difficult to admit. When Dante refused to show up, Kalagan forced me to do something I never wanted to do. I would have rather died...but I did it anyway. I agreed to that bit with the 'Varalikas,' saying that they were Leila's parents." She turned to Leila. "Kalagan's gang of clowns was going to hurt you if I didn't comply....I was trying to keep you and your dad safe." She covered her face and burst into tears. "I...I'm so ashamed."

Leila's pain was suddenly replaced with anger. It filled her like air in a balloon, and it continued to fill her until she worried she might pop. "They *did* hurt me! They pretended to be my parents!"

"They hurt you, yes, but...you're still *alive*!"

Leila wanted to push Sandra out of the shop. Out of Mineral Wells. Out of her life, her memories, the whole universe! Instead, she quietly asked, "Couldn't you have just asked for the book? Couldn't you have just told us the truth?"

Mr. Vernon simply stared at Sandra, waiting for her response.

Sandra glanced at the ledger pinned underneath Carter's arm. "Dante would not have been willing to give that book to anyone, especially not Kalagan. I don't need psychic powers to be sure of that. It's a book of names. Names of people who—"

"Enough," said Vernon fiercely, forcing Sandra to clamp her mouth shut. Then he was suddenly chirpy. "It's time for Sandra to go....Thanks for stopping by! Don't ever come again!"

"But, Dad! There's so much we need to find out. What about Kalagan?" Leila faced Sandra, her fear and anxiety tamped down. "That afternoon you were talking to yourself in the resort lounge...he was there, wasn't he? He was telling you what he needed you to do. And then from backstage, behind the curtain during your show...But you didn't want to listen."

"I—I..." Sandra started. But she couldn't seem to say more.

"Fine. Then I just have one more question for you—" Leila began.

Before she could finish, she heard a loud engine outside the shop. A tiny red clown car pulled up to the curb, and a *bang* echoed up and down the street as the exhaust pipe backfired. Pammy and Bob Varalika hopped out of the passenger side door, followed by the man they'd called Tommy, then two more kids and an adult. Last but not least, towering over them and wearing a wicked smile, was the fake lawyer himself, Mr. Sammy Falsk, Esquire.

TWENTY-
SEVEN

Before the Vernon family could bar the door, the seven former clowns entered the magic shop. They had billy clubs and wore menacing looks on their faces. A thwack from one of those weapons would have made an egg-sized knob on someone's skull. Or worse. Sammy Falsk grabbed Carter by the wrist and pulled him into a headlock. "Let him go!" Leila screamed.

"Everyone settle down," the fake lawyer barked before turning his attention to Vernon. "I'd ask how you got out of the basement, but our leader warned us you'd play with magic."

"Let the boy go," Mr. Vernon said.

"No," the thug growled.

"Who are you? What do you want?" the Other Vernon asked.

"We're the former frown clowns," Sammy sneered. "But you can call us Jimmy, Timmy, Tommy, Tammy, Sammy, Pammy, and Bob."

"Those names are as dumb as you," Carter growled.

"Shut up, kid!" Sammy snapped.

Leila sized up the intruders. Instantly, she realized that the seven villains were the same seven volunteers from Sandra's stage show at the Grand Oak. So her friends had been right—even Sandra's performance was as fake as she was.

"As you can see, we outnumber you," said Sammy. "So I recommend you cooperate. All we want is a book. Did you find the ledger, Sandra?"

Sandra shook her head. "No. But it doesn't matter. They won't give up the book. We should just leave them be."

"Whose side are you on?" asked Mrs. Varalika.

"Hand over the book, Dante," Mr. Varalika said with a threatening lilt, raising his club over Carter's head. "No one's getting out of here until that happens."

Mr. Vernon held up his hands. "Okay, okay! I'll give you what you want. Just...let him go. Don't hurt anyone."

"Give us the book," said Mrs. Varalika. "And no tricks this time! I'm allergic to smoke and fake fog!"

"Something you might want to keep secret," Leila muttered.

"Not to worry!" Mr. Vernon exclaimed. "I've got nothing up my sleeves."

"Magicians always say that," Jimmy growled. "Be sure it's true."

Leila shuddered, wishing that all this would be over. She wanted Sandra out of the store. She couldn't stand to be near such an awful liar, even if the woman was trying to help them now. Even if she might be—

Through the window, Leila noticed Theo, Ridley, and the twins heading through the park toward the store. *Oh no*, she thought. They'd all planned to meet at the shop after the appointment with the lawyer. But Theo, Ridley, Olly, and Izzy had no idea that they'd be in danger if they came across the street. Leila tried to keep her expression blank, so that the villains wouldn't turn around and see the other Misfits. She squeezed her poppa's hand and he squeezed back. He'd seen them too.

"I think my book might be in the back of the store," said Mr. Vernon. "If you'd all just follow me."

"Uh-uh," Sammy warned. "Not all of us. Mrs. Varalika, you go. And be careful. This man has fast hands."

"I'm not worried," said Mrs. V. "I've got fast *fists*." It amazed Leila how different this woman seemed from before. Leila couldn't believe she had actually thought that Mrs. Varalika might have given birth to her. Pammy stomped off behind Mr. Vernon, who seemed to glide between the shop's tables and displays as if his feet weren't even touching the floor.

Leila watched in horror as Theo, Ridley, and the twins approached the shop door. She hoped they might notice what was happening, but it was too bright outside—the other Misfits could only see their reflections in the window. The bell jangled as they entered. When the door bumped against Sammy, the tall man jumped, knocking into Tommy.

Carter broke Sammy's hold and dashed farther into the store, putting distance between himself and the villains. Leila called to her friends, "Watch out! They're the frown clowns!"

Theo, Ridley, Olly, and Izzy moved to the right,

away from the hands of Timmy and Jimmy, and into the small space behind the counter.

As soon as the door slammed shut, all chaos broke loose.

"*Grab those kids, and find the ledger!*" Sammy yelled.

The remaining frown clowns bolted forward. Olly and Izzy did a quick box-step-and-bow, blocking Mr. Varalika. As they leaned toward him, the two field mice jumped from their vest pockets onto his jacket lapels. Mr. Varalika turned white and let out a bloodcurdling shriek. He ran smack into Sammy's chest. The two former clowns beat at each other as the mice ran an obstacle course across their bodies, hopping from slapping hands to raised knees to kicking feet.

Both twins cried out, "*Yay!*" They were impressed that their mice had finally managed to do a trick, even if it was one they'd never trained for.

"Go, *Ozzy*!" shouted Olly.

"Get him, *Illy*!" Izzy cheered.

(Phew! I finally got those names right!)

But then the mice dropped out of sight, and the two men were left alone, looking sheepishly down at the twins. Sammy squinted and growled, "You'll pay for that."

The twins clasped arms. Olly barrel-rolled over Izzy, kicking his legs in the air, smacking both men across their faces with the shiny tips of his leather tap shoes. The villains flailed and knocked over a stack of windup chatter-teeth, which tumbled to the floor. Tiny jaws hopped, snapping at their feet. Olly landed perfectly and then bolted toward one side of the store. Izzy dashed away toward the other. The men shook off the kicks to their heads and then sprinted after the two—Sammy toward Olly, Varalika toward Izzy.

Meanwhile, Theo and Ridley moved farther into the store, but neither got very far. Tammy crawled out from under a display table in front of Ridley and stuck a billy club between the spokes of her wheel. Ridley's chair bucked, nearly tossing her onto the floor. "Don't touch my chair!" Ridley yelled. Then she smiled and added, "Wanna see an amazing trick?" The girl was so startled by the offer that she actually paused and looked up at Ridley, wide-eyed.

Ridley plucked three brass rings from the display table. "Look! Totally separate. Totally solid!" She spun the rings in her fists and then clanked them together. Tammy blanched at the sound. When Ridley spread the rings out again, they were latched together. "Things aren't always what they seem, kid." She lined the rings up again and tossed them over the small girl's head and shoulders. They slid down and pinned the girl's arms to her body. Tammy shrieked and squirmed and toppled over, unable to move. Ridley started trying to extract the club from her wheel.

A few feet away, Tommy was swinging his billy club and stomping toward Theo. In retreat, Theo jumped up onto a separate display table, kicked aside several books, and whipped his magic violin bow out of his pants pocket. He held it like a wizard's wand toward the small, grinning man. "Do not come closer," Theo said. "I'm warning you! I have secret powers you *do not* wish to observe." Tommy dipped under the table and was gone from view. "Shoot," Theo whispered to himself, trying to peer over the edge for a glimpse of him.

Across the store, Leila and the Other Mr. Vernon huddled in the center of the room, overwhelmed by the commotion. Sandra watched them, frozen near the front window. When Top Hat jumped out from behind a glass jar filled with feather flowers, Sandra released a surprised peep. She dropped to her hands and knees before crawling around the side of a bookcase. Leila tried to go after her, but her poppa hugged her close.

Near the rear of the shop, Mrs. Varalika clutched Vernon's elbow, digging long fingernails through his jacket and into his skin. The bookshelf in the back wall suddenly swung open, and Carter popped out, startling the woman. He raised both arms slowly, dramatically, and before Mrs. Varalika could scream, several decks of cards burst forth from his palms, shooting at her wildly, their sharp edges nicking her face.

It was all the distraction that Mr. Vernon needed. Leila blinked, and her dad was no longer at the woman's side. He'd stepped onto the secret lift that was embedded into one of the columns below the balcony and zipped up and over the railing.

The flurry of cards knocked Mrs. Varalika off her feet, and she fell toward the bookcase, pulling one shelf loose. When she hit the floor, several of the heaviest volumes thumped down on top of her.

A moment later, Vernon appeared at the balcony railing, holding a length of white rope. "Catch!" he called, tossing it down to Leila, who caught it one-handed.

Timmy careened toward her, arms outstretched as if to catch her and hold her hostage. Quickly, Leila handed one end of the rope to her poppa. Together, they pulled it taut and dashed at Timmy, clotheslining him so he flew backward and crashed onto his back.

"You all right?" Leila asked her poppa. But before he could answer, Timmy jumped to his feet again and knocked her poppa to the floor. Timmy raised his fists and was about to bring them down hard. As fast as a whip, Leila turned the rope into a lasso and caught the villain's fists. She gave one jerk, pulling the man backward. When he tried to reach for Leila, she looped the rope around his wrists twice, then dove between his legs and wrapped the rope around one, pulling it taut. Timmy crashed to the floor, and Leila knotted the rope. It was the perfect trap. The more Timmy pulled, the tighter the rope got. His wrists and one leg were clasped together in an impenetrable knot. "Sammy!" he cried out. "She got me! I'm done for!"

Sammy was busy, though—he was holding Olly by the collar, having finally snagged the boy. Olly whined and looked around for Izzy. "Do you like balloon animals?" Sammy asked, reaching into his jacket and removing several brightly colored balloons. "I make a *killer* giraffe." He blew the balloons up quickly like a pro, then held them near Olly's ear and squeezed them. They burst all at once, sounding like fireworks in the small shop. Olly cringed and then fell to the floor, clutching at his ears. Sammy glanced around the shop. "Anyone have eyes on that ledger yet?"

"Workin' on it," came a raspy voice from the spiral staircase. The stout woman who called herself Jimmy walked slowly but solidly up the steps.

"Leila!" Vernon shouted from the balcony. "Run and get help!"

"I can't leave you here with them," said Leila.

"We *are* the help, Mr. Vernon!" Theo shouted from atop the display table, raising his magic violin bow. He turned to find Tommy leaping toward him. Calmly, Theo positioned the bow over a box of Mexican jumping beans near his feet. The box rose up off the table and tipped over. The little beans fell to the floor in a giant twitching, hopping mass. Tommy grinned and kicked them away. The small man clutched the edge of the table and began to shake it, trying to knock Theo off balance.

Leila leapfrogged over the counter, then ducked down and started digging through boxes, searching for what might save them all. Handcuffs!

"I warned you," said Theo, moving the violin bow over Tommy's head. With a twist of Theo's wrist, the small man suddenly lifted several inches off the floor. He screeched in surprise. Theo steadied his feet, moving the bow away from the edge of the table and out of Tommy's grip. The little man was stuck, dangling just above the floor. And Theo looked like he was conducting a symphony. "Your schemes are rotten—just like your *ridiculous rhyming* names!"

Sammy shouted, "Jimmy! Varalika! Hurry, Vernon is up to no good!"

But then, the same could be said for Jimmy. She'd finally reached the balcony and was chugging toward Mr. Vernon, who was backed into a corner. From the wide pocket of her green dress, she removed a giant clown-makeup compact and flipped it open, revealing a powder puff of extraordinary girth. White powder spilled out as she gripped the puff in her thick fingers. She rushed at Vernon and slapped at his face, enveloping him in clouds of choking dust. Mr. Vernon coughed and raised an arm, trying to block her, but she just kept coming, like a steam engine on a straight track.

Ridley noticed Mr. Varalika cornering Izzy near the hat rack. He was holding a large sword that Ridley recognized from the glass case underneath the front counter. Izzy looked like she was playing a complicated game of patty-cake, slapping at the man every time he moved toward her, but Varalika wasn't giving up.

With one last punch, Ridley finally knocked the billy club loose from her chair. The club skittered across the floor, just missing Tammy's cute little nose. Still unable to do anything but roll around, the girl screeched in anger.

Ridley grasped her wheels and pushed as hard as she could. The chair flew forward, right into the back of Mr. Varalika's legs. His knees buckled as Ridley swiveled out of his way, then he crumpled to the floor, writhing in pain. The sword dropped with a resonant clatter.

Izzy cheered, but then her eyes grew wide. Ridley noticed a large shadow cast on the wall; someone was looming behind her chair. She shifted her elbow toward one of her armrests and pressed a secret button. Water squirted out from her handlebars, catching Sammy in the eyes. He stumbled backward with a roar of frustration. Ridley spun and knocked him in the shins with her leg-rests. He shrieked in agony and stumbled away from her. "You don't mess with a girl and her chair!" she spat.

Izzy saw Olly on the floor on the opposite side of the store. She ran over to him and cradled his head, whispering into his ear.

Leila noticed her dad on the balcony, struggling with Jimmy's powder puff, fending her off with his sharp elbows. Trying to focus, she rifled through the drawers behind the counter. Where were those darn handcuffs?

"Would...you...*please*...*stop doing that!*" Mr. Vernon choked out between Jimmy's powder attacks. The woman launched herself from another angle, but she lost her balance and stumbled into the railing. There was a snap and a cracking sound as the wood shattered, and her body crashed through the banister and over the edge of the balcony. She landed with a tremendous *whump* on Mr. Varalika below.

Mr. Varalika crawled out from underneath Jimmy. He noticed the twins unattended and struggled to his feet, but the Other Mr. Vernon blocked his path, towering over the villain. "Oh no you don't." The Other Mr. Vernon removed a small paper packet, folded just so, from his pants pocket. He tore it open and poured red powder into the palm of his hand. "Do you like it *spicy*?" he asked. Not waiting for an answer, he blew the red powder directly into Varalika's face. Varalika howled and dropped to the floor again, sneezing and rubbing at his burning eyes.

Seeing that his group was losing, Sammy gathered his bearings, then rushed to snatch up the fallen sword.

Mr. Vernon called out a distraction, using classic misdirection: "Looking for this?" He held a ledger with a marbleized cover over the railing. Sammy ran up the stairs, sword in hand.

"Over here!" Carter stepped out from behind one

of the freestanding bookshelves. Mr. Vernon tossed him the ledger. Sammy turned and raced for it, but before he could make contact, the book seemed to disappear from Carter's hands.

"Look what I found!" said Theo from atop the display table. Now he was the one holding the ledger. He let go of it, but the book continued to float in front of him, spinning slowly, hypnotically, several feet above the spot where Tommy was doing something similar.

Ridley zoomed by him and snatched the ledger from the air. She raced down the aisle in her chair, as if daring the villain to play a game of chicken. He stepped frantically out of her way, but she managed to whack him with the ledger as she passed.

"Enough!" Sammy shouted. He was the only frown clown still standing. Clutching the sword, he spun and leapt in front of Ridley's chair, stopping it with his foot. Ridley jerked forward, nearly tumbling from her seat again.

Sammy snatched the ledger from Ridley's hands and quickly opened the cover. His face turned purple as he saw what was inside: an illustrated volume of simple magic tricks. The title at the top of the open page was *Magic for Morons!* Ridley chuckled and tried to back her chair away, but Sammy threw the book to the floor and stomped on one wheel, holding her in place. He raised the sword and pointed it at Ridley's chest. "If you don't give us that book within the next three seconds," he called up to Mr. Vernon, "you're going to be *very* sorry."

Leila rose from behind the counter. She'd finally found what she'd been looking for.

"One!" Sammy shouted. The Misfits froze. "Two!"

Leila glanced up at her dad, who shook his head at her, as if he didn't want her to move. "Three!"

Sammy shoved the sword toward Ridley's sternum as a sudden blur of movement appeared behind him, and a loud *thwack* echoed throughout the magic shop. The man dropped to the floor like a sack of marbles.

Sandra stood over the unconscious Sammy holding a glimmering object. It was her large purse, the one with the crystal ball embroidered on it. Sandra reached inside and pulled out an *actual* crystal ball.

She glanced at Jimmy, who was trying to get up, and yelled at her, "Any sudden moves, and I predict a very painful future."

Presto landed on the broken balcony railing. She said, "*Painful future!*"

Sandra reached out to Leila. Unable to process everything that had happened, Leila didn't know what else to do. She pulled Sandra's wrist down toward Sammy's and cuffed them together, then rolled out of sight.

By the time Sandra noticed the handcuffs trapping her, Leila had managed to click two more pairs around little Tammy's and Tommy's ankles. She tossed a pair of cuffs to Carter, who attached them to Mr. and Mrs. Varalika. A final pair went to her poppa, who latched

Jimmy's and Timmy's wrists together. Mr. Varalika's eyes were still swollen, and he called out pathetically, "We are going to do *very bad things to all of you* if you don't let us go this instant."

Ridley picked up the fallen sword and pressed the tip of the blade into her hand, showing everyone how it retracted into itself. "I'm okay! Sword's a fake!" She wiped sweat from her forehead, then whispered it again to herself: "Sword's a fake...."

Carter, Theo, and Leila gathered by Ridley's chair, asking if she was all right. Of course, Ridley groaned, "I already told you I'm fine!" Izzy stumbled over with Olly, who looked like he would soon recover from the balloon blast. Ridley reached into the secret compartment in her chair's armrest and removed several small sterile-wrapped bandages. "But what about the rest of you? Who needs a Band-Aid?"

Seconds later, both Mr. Vernons gathered Leila and Carter up in their arms. White clown powder lingered in the air, like smoke after a battle.

The group listened as the sound of sirens outside grew louder and louder.

TWENTY-EIGHT

When everyone was gone and the sun started to sink once more in the sky, the Vernons began to clean the shop.

Leila and Carter crept back down to the basement. Behind the velvet curtain, he pushed the rusted door shut, and she used the club-shaped side of the skeleton key to turn the lock once and for all.

The next morning came like a jolt, and Leila woke with a start.

She asked her dad to walk with her to the town jail. She needed to speak with Sandra Santos face-to-face.

The police station and jailhouse were across the

park and down a couple blocks near the town hall. Leila forced herself to put a briskness into her step, and she held her chin up high, even when people on the street gave her funny looks. Word must have already spread about what had happened to the illustrious Madame Esmeralda. "Good morning!" she said with cheer to these people, trying to get back to her old self. It felt like flipping a switch. Well, a switch that was attached to a flickering bulb.

Mr. Vernon walked beside her, commenting on the brightness of the sky and the birdsong and the music of the trains rumbling from across town. Leila knew he was talking simply to fill the space between them, and right now, she didn't mind. She was certain that if he were to bring up anything important, she'd spill her own suspicions and plans, and, old self or new, that was something she was not ready to do.

At the jailhouse steps, Leila asked her dad if she could go inside alone. He looked surprised but nodded, holding out a white-gloved hand as if to show her the way forward. A deputy brought Leila down a long hallway to a cell that was lit only by a sliver of a window. And over the window was a row of thick black bars stuck into the stone wall.

"Miss Santos, you've got a visitor."

Sandra sat up from the cot against the wall. Her white star-shaped earrings were tangled in her long, frizzy hair. When she realized who had come to see her, she covered her face and shook her head. "Leila," she murmured through her fingers, "go home. This is no place for a girl like you."

"A girl like me? And what kind of girl is that?" Leila said, her voice steady and strong, though inside she knew it was about to crack. "I'm more than just a smiling face and a supportive friend. I'm more than what people think they see."

Sandra glanced at the deputy and nodded. He turned and left them alone.

"I've come for answers," said Leila. "And I don't mean any psychic mumbo jumbo—where you make me look inside myself and realize the stuff I already know. I'm talking *facts*."

Sandra sighed. "What facts do you wish to know?"

"Promise you'll tell me the truth?"

"I'll do my best."

"Why did you do it? Why did you come here?"

"I thought I explained all that to you yesterday."

"Right. That Kalagan person...and my dad's book." Leila squinted, trying to read Sandra. The woman seemed

lost today. Defeated. And not just by the Magic Misfits...
There was something else going on in her mind. Something...*deeper*. Locked and chained down. It was the secret
that Leila had come to discover. "You said that Kalagan
is a mesmerist. He's good at making people do stuff they
don't want to do. I guess that means you wouldn't have
returned to Mineral Wells if not for him?"

Sandra's eyes went cold. "No. I don't suppose I ever
would have." She was hiding something. Something
she didn't want to face.

"So then, he hypnotized you?"

"Could have." Her voice shrank to a croak.

"I don't believe that," said Leila. "I think you've
wanted to come back to Mineral Wells for a very long
time." Sandra didn't answer. "I think there was something here that you wanted to see for yourself...some-
thing that had nothing to do with Kalagan or the old
Emerald Ring." Now Sandra turned away, hanging
her head and hugging herself. "I know that you never
wanted to hurt anyone, Sandra. But especially not *me*.
For all the scheming and all the planning, I believe
that I matter to you. I could see it in your eyes the
moment we met. And you tried to pass along clues that
at first I didn't understand. Things you were trying to

tell me but couldn't flat-out say—the biggest one being your 'prediction' at dinner about how important my key would be in the coming days. You knew I might need it to get out through the tunnels." Leila tried to gulp down the dryness in her throat. "The big question is how you knew that I had the key to begin with."

Sandra answered without looking up. "I'm psychic, remember?"

"Psychic or not...I think there's another reason you knew about it." Trembling, Leila lifted the string from around her neck and let it dangle in front of the bars of the cell. "And I think the reason is that you're the one who gave it to me in the first place." Sandra stiffened. Turning her head slowly, she met Leila's gaze. Her eyes were red and watery. Leila bit her bottom lip to keep it from quivering. She refused to cry about this. Not now. Not ever. "You're my birth mother. Aren't you?"

Sandra didn't speak for almost a minute.

For Leila, it felt like eternity.

Finally, Sandra nodded. She stood and came over to the cage door. She reached out for Leila's hand, but Leila didn't give it to her, and Sandra quickly withdrew.

"You knew I was here all along? With the Vernons?" Leila asked.

"I got word that Dante had adopted you. It was... everything I could have wished for."

"Why did you leave me at Mother Margaret's? Didn't you want me?"

"Oh, I did want you, child. But it wasn't possible.... You see, Kalagan..."

"Kalagan *what*?!" Leila found herself suddenly shouting. "He hypnotized you back *then* too?"

Sandra was shaking now. "Remember the story Mrs. Varalika told on stage during the show? I made her practice those lines over and over. Because the story belongs to me."

"I—I don't know what to think."

"Back then," Sandra went on, "I couldn't afford to give you what you needed. Someone I trusted—"

"Kalagan," Leila whispered.

"I was talked into giving you away. I didn't want to, but I was made to believe it was what was best for *you*. It was the biggest mistake of my life."

Leila sniffed. "Is all that the truth or is it a lie? Are you still playing games with me, just like you used to play with the Emerald Ring?"

"Decisions we make as we get older aren't so black and white, Leila. Sometimes, there is smoke and mirrors. It's easy to get confused. And some people, like Kalagan, are good at using that confusion for their own benefit. I...I've wondered about you every day." Her eyes grew wide and her lip trembled. "I left that key in your bassinet in the hope that you would eventually wonder about me too."

Leila stepped backward. "I don't know if I can believe *anything* you say."

"I understand. I've lied to you. Belief takes trust. It takes faith. If I ever get out of here"—she indicated the dank cell—"I hope I can make you believe me."

"Are you in lots of trouble?" Leila asked. Sandra nodded. "With the police...or with Kalagan?"

"That's my smart girl: looking at all the different angles. It's what we used to practice during Emerald Ring meetings. There are so many ways to read an audience and to gauge risk and to prepare for the unexpected."

Leila couldn't help smiling. "You didn't answer my question."

Sandra blinked slowly. "I'm in *lots* of trouble. But that's not anything you should worry about."

"Is Kalagan here in Mineral Wells?" Leila asked. "Do we need to look out for him?"

Then Sandra did something strange. She opened

her mouth to speak, but no words came out. She stared at Leila as if she were surprised. "I'm sorry....I can't..."

Whether it was the mesmerist's power over Sandra's mind or Sandra's own fear that was tying her tongue down, on that day, Leila would not learn who Kalagan really was.

(And, my curious friends, I'm sorry to say that neither will you...not now anyway.)

"Good-bye, Sandra," Leila whispered. "I wish that we..." Leila's voice faded. She knew the woman was still under someone's control. Until that control was broken, Leila understood that they could never really know each other.

The skeleton key swung from Leila's clenched fist. Back and forth, back and forth. A mesmerist's pendulum. Leila kept her voice low when she said, "My dad told me that your father was the locksmith for the whole town." Sandra nodded. "That means he probably built this very jail cell."

Sandra smiled at the thought of her father. "It's very likely that he did."

Leila lowered the key into Sandra's hand.

"Then it may unlock your cell. Do what you think is right," Leila whispered, backing away. "But please... just wait until I'm gone."

TWENTY-NINE

Leila found Mr. Vernon waiting for her just around the corner from the cell. She asked him, "Did you hear everything?" The way he squeezed her hand told her the answer was yes.

On the way home, they talked about real things, no longer shackled by secrets and fear.

"Was it bad that I gave her my skeleton key?" Leila asked.

Mr. Vernon thought for half a second. "It was hers to begin with. Let her do with it what she will."

"Unlike Bosso," Leila added, "Sandra has a con-science. I don't think we have anything to worry about."

"Not from Sandra anyway," Vernon added, though under his breath. They walked in silence for a few seconds. Then, for the first time ever, Leila heard him stammer. "I—I know what you're thinking."

Feeling nervous, Leila teased to lighten the mood. "Please don't tell me you're psychic now too!"

"Hardly." He paused and then smiled down at her. "At least, I hope I'm not. Knowing the future doesn't appear to be the most *useful* skill for a magician." He reached into his jacket pocket and pulled out a black wand with white tips. As he moved his hands apart, the wand began to float between them. "Not like levitation." He clapped his hands together. The wand became a thick black billy club, which he clutched in his fist. "Or transformation." He blew into the end of the club, and before Leila could blink, it had disappeared. "Or vanishing." He held his empty hand out to her.

"Or escape!" Leila added with a skip and a playful twirl away from him. "So tell me, Dad. What *am* I thinking?"

"Ah yes," he said, holding up a finger. "You are wondering if I knew who you were when I first met you at Mother Margaret's."

"I guess I *was* wondering that," said Leila. "And?"

"The answer is...no. And *yes*."

Confused, Leila shook her head.

"During our magic tour all those years ago, when I performed the charity show for the children at Mother Margaret's, your enthusiasm caught my attention from the back of the room. And afterward, when we spoke, your sparkly eyes made me think of an old friend."

"Sandra?" Leila swung his hand as they crossed the street.

He nodded. "I'd been traveling far and wide, learning new magic skills, making friends, performing wherever I could while discovering the good in the world. By that time, I'd lost touch with Sandra, so I'd never learned that she'd given birth to a baby girl. And I certainly had no clue that she'd left that baby girl in the care of others. So when I met you, it was my memory of Sandra that made me curious to know more, but it was your spirit—my tough and clever girl—*your* spirit that captured your poppa's and my hearts. I cherish the memory of the day we brought you home. I wouldn't trade it for the biggest slice of pie in Mineral Wells."

Leila raised an eyebrow. "Not even lemon meringue?"

"Not even lemon meringue."

"Mmm," said Leila. "Pie sounds really good right now."

And with that, they decided to stop at the Main Street Diner for a sweet treat.

★ ★ ★

When they were nearly back at the magic shop, Leila was surprised to find Carter crouched on the sidewalk, holding on to one end of a white string. The other end was looped around the body of a little blond monkey. Carter was handing the creature stacks of shortbread cookies that he was producing from thin air. The monkey seemed happy to oblige, shoving each shortbread into his wide mouth.

Leila raced across the street, being sure to check for traffic, then skidded to a halt and dropped to her knees. "Where did you find him?!"

"Creeping around under the gazebo in the town green," Carter answered. "I lured him out with these treats and managed to slip your harness around him."

"Oh, he's sooo cute!" Leila squeaked. Seeing the monkey was almost enough to make her forget about her awful morning.

Mr. Vernon held his palms against his forehead. "I don't suppose you've called animal control, have you, Carter?"

"Aw, Dad, can't we keep him?" Leila begged.

Mr. Vernon closed his eyes and sighed. He seemed to know how this would end.

Carter chimed in, making his blue eyes big and innocent. "Bosso's locked up along with the frown clowns and the rest of the circus crew. The monkey is an orphan."

"Just like we used to be," said Leila. "How could we send him away? Doesn't he deserve love like the rest of us?" Mr. Vernon was listening, and Leila sensed he was about to break. "Besides! Imagine how much more foot traffic a real-live monkey would bring into the store!"

Mr. Vernon sighed. "I'll have to check with Poppa. But *maybe* we can give the little beast a trial run."

"Brilliant!" Carter cried. "I've already thought of the perfect name."

"Oh really?" asked Leila. "What were you thinking?"

"Well, you already have a parrot named Presto.

It would only be fitting if she had a monkey sibling named Change-O." At that, the monkey glanced up at all three of them and shook its head as if in opposition to the name. Carter laughed, before remembering his friend. "How did everything go?" he asked Leila.

"Come inside, and I'll tell you."

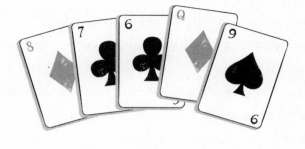

THIRTY

A week later, the Magic Misfits met once again at the magic shop. Mr. Vernon watched over them from his spot behind the counter.

Presto sat on her perch, while Change-O, the monkey, was busy snacking from a bowl of seeds and nuts that the Other Mr. Vernon had put together. The monkey had settled down significantly since Carter had first brought him into the building. Change-O had even gotten used to his new harness and leash, and Carter was trying to teach him the concept of palming shortbread cookies.

Of course, Change-O kept eating them.

"It's so nice to have everyone together again," said Leila.

Carter added, "Especially without a gang of clowns trying to beat us up."

"Even our parents couldn't keep us away," said Ridley.

"What would Mineral Wells *do* without the Magic Misfits?" asked Theo.

"Izzy and I *had* to come back!" said Olly.

"Yeah," said Izzy. "We needed to find our mice." The twins pulled their pets from their vest pockets and held them next to each other. "And they already know a new trick!"

"Oh really?" asked Ridley, sounding unconvinced. "Which one?"

"They read each other's minds!"

The Misfits chuckled, but the twins continued. "You can do it, Ozzy!"

"Concentrate, Illy!"

The mice stared at each other, sniffed at the air, and squeaked.

"They're getting really good," Olly concluded. "If only we knew what they were saying to each other!"

"We heard that Sandra disappeared from the jail-house," Theo said to Leila. "Are you scared that she'll return?"

Leila glanced at Mr. Vernon for help. She wasn't ready to share what she'd figured out about Sandra. Carter looked at Leila, his knowing eyes hinting that he was in on the secret too. She smiled, and after a moment he nodded, sensitive enough to understand that the secret belonged to her. And only her. None of the others seemed to notice. Leila simply smiled and said, "No. I'm not scared anymore."

"If there's one thing that the showdown with the frown clowns was good for," said Ridley, "it was practicing our tricks!"

"What I want to know," said Theo, "is what was in the book that Sandra needed so badly?"

"And where was it hidden?" asked Izzy.

Mr. Vernon grinned. "I find that the best hiding spots are in plain sight."

"Plain Sight?" Olly repeated. "Isn't that a town up north?" Izzy elbowed his side and shushed him.

Mr. Vernon shook his head and then reached behind the counter. He pulled out one of his business ledgers. It looked like the same book the Misfits had tossed around the shop during the brawl with the frown clowns. The marbleized cover was made of flimsy cardboard. It didn't look important at all—it certainly didn't seem like something that a criminal organization would desperately want to get their hands on. He opened the cover and flipped through the pages. The item descriptions and prices and dates of sales—all written in many columns with mind-numbing precision—were the same as the first time he'd shown the notebook to Leila and Carter, on the night Change-O had tried to steal it.

"What is it?" asked Carter.

Mr. Vernon backed away from the counter, giving the Misfits space to crowd around the book. "Look closer. Do you really need me to say that things aren't always as they seem?"

"Another code," Ridley said. Mr. Vernon tipped his top hat at her.

"What does it mean?" asked Theo.

"Sandra was right," Mr. Vernon went on. "My little book here hides a list of names. Names that Kalagan would do most anything to learn."

"Whose names?" Carter asked. "Your family?"

"Not far off. More like…a *club*."

"You're in another secret club?" asked Izzy. "Tell us!"

Mr. Vernon laughed, tearing a sheet out from the back of the notebook. "It's an organization for modern magicians. And just like your club, its members use magic for only benevolent purposes, never for malicious self-gain. However, I've learned recently how extremely important it is that their names remain secret." He tore the page in half, once, twice, three times. Then he crumpled the page in his fist. "Because *another* club is out there, hiding in the shadows of small towns all around this country, a bad club, who use magic to benefit only themselves. This bad club wants to get their hands on those names, so that they can make the good magicians change their minds."

"Kalagan is part of the bad club?" asked Leila. "The true leader?"

He nodded, and then added more seriously, "In time I'll expound on the topic. But for now..." He blinked and then cleared his throat. "For now, I'd suggest that you all keep practicing. Magic should be used to make people smile. But you never know when you might need those skills for...something else."

"To help people," said Carter.

"*To help people*," Mr. Vernon echoed, sounding a bit

like Presto. He opened his fist and removed the crumpled pieces of ledger paper. But when he smoothed them out on the counter, the paper had become whole again. Olly and Izzy nearly fell down in shock.

Leila whispered in her dad's ear, "Thank you for telling us all that. It means a lot to me."

"You're welcome, Leila."

The Other Mr. Vernon appeared on the balcony wearing his chef uniform. He called out, "I'm late for work," before quickly descending the stairs.

Leila caught him as he leaned in to give her a kiss good-bye. She took both her fathers' hands and pulled them into a hug. "I'm so glad you chose to be my parents," she whispered.

The men leaned back and looked at each other in surprise. Then they both knelt and kissed Leila's forehead. "Oh, Leila," said her poppa. "That's not exactly how it happened."

Her dad shook his head. "We all chose one another," said Mr. Vernon. "And we couldn't be happier about it."

After another brief squeeze, her poppa rose and waved farewell to everyone. Blowing a kiss to Leila, he closed the door of the magic shop behind him.

The Misfits were already heading toward the secret room at the back of the shop, the leashed monkey in tow. Theo called out, "Leila, come on! I've been working on something that I want to show you. Hopefully we can incorporate it into our next performance."

"Our *next* performance?" Carter asked. "But when's that going to be?"

"Who knows?" said Ridley. "The point is we all

need to be ready." The group disappeared through the doorway in the bookcase.

Mr. Vernon shooed Leila away. "Go on. I've got some work to do myself."

As Leila made her way across the room, she reached for the key on the string around her neck, but then she remembered that it was gone now. And in that moment, she felt a strange twinge right in the center of her chest. It wasn't anything so mysterious as the psychic premonitions that Sandra had claimed to experience—more like a tiny spark of hope that one day her fondest treasure would return to her.

For now, she understood that what mattered most was in the secret room at the back of her father's magic shop.

HOW TO...

Make a Rope Indestructible

You didn't think I'd let you go without showing you one of Theo's favorite rope tricks, did you? One of the most satisfying things a magician can do is to make it look like something has been ruined—then, with a flash and a smile, show the audience that all has been set right again.

Just like in our story! After everything that went wrong for Leila in the preceding pages, who would've imagined that she'd get her happy ending?

Oh, you did? Well, then, I stand corrected.

In this trick, you'll amaze your friends by cutting a piece of rope in half and then restoring it to its original size. If you do this one correctly and with a bit of finesse, your friends will gawp at you, wondering where you got your astounding magical powers. You can tell them it was from me. I don't mind.

WHAT YOU'LL NEED:

A length of white rope (You can use string if you must.)
A pair of scissors
A volunteer

SECRET MAGIC MOVE:

Before you start the trick, bunch up a large amount of the rope and hide it inside your left fist.

STEPS:

1. Allow the tip of the rope to stick up from the top of your left hand and the bottom of the rope to dangle loosely below. (About a foot and a half of rope should hang.)

2. With your right hand, grab the bottom of the rope and bring it up so that it is even with the tip of the rope in your left hand. The rope will loop down.

3. Ask a volunteer from the audience to use the scissors and cut the rope at the bottom of the loop.

4. Move your hands apart and show the audience that you are now holding two pieces of rope that appear to be the same size.

(*Magic Secret:* Except they are not the same size, remember? There is still a bunch of rope hidden in your left fist!)

5. Tell your audience that you shall now attempt to restore the two pieces of rope.

6. Bring your hands together and shove the shorter piece into your right fist.

7. Speak some magic words to help heal the rope! *Ala-ka-blab-ra!* Or whatever you like!

8. Keeping the shorter piece hidden in your *right* fist, use your right forefinger and thumb to pinch the piece from your left hand and then extend it slowly, pulling the hidden rope from your *left* fist until it is fully revealed.

9. Hold up your left hand, showing the audience a piece of rope that looks like it has been restored to its original length.

SECRET MAGIC MOVE:

Drop your right hand out of sight, or maybe even slip the shorter rope into your pocket while everyone is focused on the longer rope. Misdirection fools them again!

10. After lots of practice, you'll have acquired yet another trick to put into your now hefty-looking bag. Take your well-earned bow!

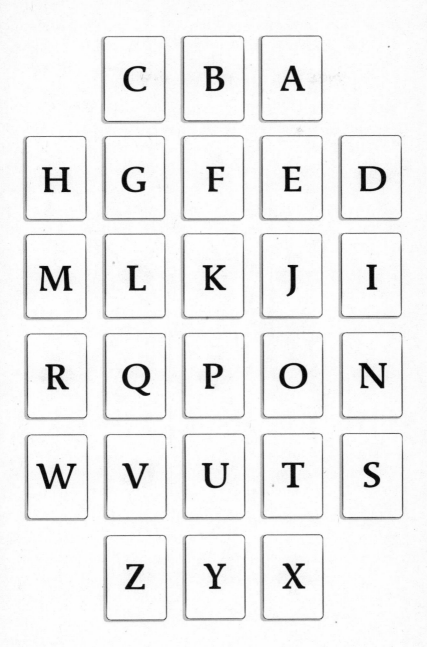

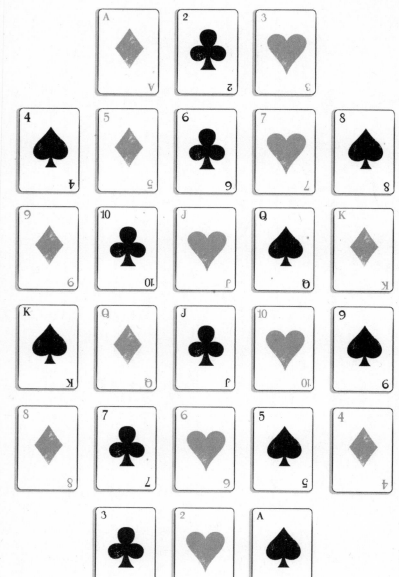

— WHAT'S MORSE CODE? —

Check it out for yourself!

A	•—	O	———	0	—————
B	—•••	P	•——•	1	•————
C	—•—•	Q	——•—	2	••———
D	—••	R	•—•	3	•••——
E	•	S	•••	4	••••—
F	••—•	T	—	5	•••••
G	——•	U	••—	6	—••••
H	••••	V	•••—	7	——•••
I	••	W	•——	8	———••
J	•———	X	—••—	9	————•
K	—•—	Y	—•——	period	•—•—•—
L	•—••	Z	——••	comma	——••——
M	——			question mark	••——••
N	—•				

A PROMISE TO RETURN

I'm so happy you stuck with me through the end of another book, but you should probably know that the adventures of the Magic Misfits are far from over. In the coming tales, our heroes will encounter new dangers that create confusion, chaos, and a little bit of havoc! If havoc is something you're interested in, be sure to return to Mineral Wells with me. You might even learn a few more tricks along the way! But for now, it's time to *practice, practice, practice* the ones you've already learned.

Speaking of which, I've got one final magical lesson. When someone asks you what it means to *escape*, I hope you're clever enough to share with them that it's not just about lockpicks and rope tricks and getting away from treacherous villains.

Remember: A story can be an escape from an ordinary life. A happy memory can be an escape from an unpleasant present. A game with friends is like an escape from boredom. And being part of a club is an escape from loneliness. The Magic Misfits know this firsthand, and now...*so do you!*

Now, get out there and tell a story.

Reminisce.

Play a game.

Join a club.

*Disappear, transform, levitate, escape....*Show your friends what you can do! Who knows? You might just inspire them to make a little bit of magic.

— — — — — — — — — — —.

— — — — — — — — — — —

— — — — — — — — — — —

— — — — — — — — — — —

— — — — — — — — — — —,

— — — — — — — — —

— — — — — — — — — — —

— — — — — — — — — — —.

— — — — — — — — — — — —,

— — — — — — —

— — — — — — —, — — — — —

— — — —. — — — — — — — — —

— — — — — — — — — — — —

— — — — —!

ACKNOWLEDGMENTS

Please refer to Book One. I still feel the same way about all of those helpful people, and it seems a waste of ink to repeat here.

Neil Patrick Harris is an accomplished actor, producer, director, host, and author. Harris served as president of the Academy of Magical Arts from 2011 to 2014. He lives in Harlem, New York, with his husband, David, their twins, Gideon and Harper, and two hilarious dogs named Watson and Gidget.

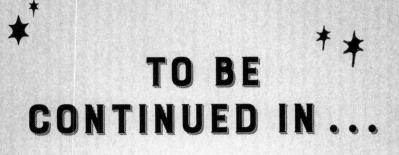

TO BE
CONTINUED IN ...

Step right up,

girls and boys, ladies and gents!

Have I got a

~~tall~~

~~short~~

just-the-right-height tale for you....

This never-before-seen-or-heard story is

FOR BARNES & NOBLE READERS ONLY!

Turn the page for an exclusive lost chapter

featuring Magic Misfit twins

Olly & Izzy Golden in...

THE TWIN TREASURE HUNT

THE TWIN TREASURE HUNT

"I need an adventure!" Olly announced.

"*Déjà vu*," Izzy said to her twin brother.

"Gesundheit!" Olly said, handing his twin sister his handkerchief. "I hope you're not coming down with a cold."

Izzy rolled her eyes. "I didn't sneeze, weirdo. I said *déjà vu*, as in I had a feeling you've said that exact thing before."

"Unlikely," Olly said.

It was a warm Sunday morning in the sleepy town of Mineral Wells. Similarly dressed twins Olly and Izzy Golden were sitting on the wall outside the Grand Oak Resort, which also happened to be their home.

"Seriously, though, I'm bored stiff. I'm as bored as"—Olly thought a moment—"a wooden board?"

"As metaphors go, that was pretty weak," Izzy said, "but I agree. After one single-handedly takes down a bunch of thieves for a *second* time, it's hard to return to normal life."

"Single-handedly? You wish," Olly snipped. "You couldn't have done it without me."

"Double-handedly, then," Izzy said.

"Actually, we each have both our hands, meaning four hands were used. Wouldn't that be quadruple-handedly?"

"Well, technically, the other Misfits helped. And since there's six of us, all with two hands each, that'd make us…"

"Twelve-tuple-handedly?" Olly guessed.

"The word you're searching for is twelvefold, or *duo-decuple*," a scratchy voice sounded from behind them. The twins jumped, having thought they were alone.

"Yeesh! Don't you know not to sneak up on people like that, Dean?!" Izzy growled at the frail and wrinkly old man standing behind them. "You could give a girl a heart attack."

The Grand Oak Resort bellhop chuckled. "I apologize. I didn't mean to frighten you."

"I wasn't scared…" Olly said, before adding in a whisper, "…much."

"What are you up to?" Izzy asked the older gentleman.

"Making sure all is well on the eastern front," he

said. "And keeping my eyes peeled for…never mind. I'm sure you don't want to hear about the possibility of hidden treasure. I'm certain you have far better things to do with your time."

Olly and Izzy looked at each other intently, knowing that they were both thinking the exact same thing at the exact same time. They turned to Dean and shouted, "Tell us everything!"

Dean offered a sly smile. "Rumor has it that there's treasure hidden here at the Grand Oak Resort."

"Pirate treasure?" Olly asked exuberantly.

"A barrel of cash?" Izzy asked excitedly.

"Bricks of gold?" Olly asked enthusiastically.

"Royal jewels?" Izzy asked eagerly.

"Not quite any of those," Dean said. "But a treasure far more valuable—to those who know what to do with it."

"Oooooh," the twins cooed. "So how do we find it?"

Dean surveyed the area to make sure they were alone. "With this…" he said, retrieving an old piece of parchment from his pocket. It had been handled so often, the thick paper had become as soft as a silk scarf.

"Unfortunately, it's all in code." Dean the Bellhop frowned. "Without the cipher, I suppose I should just give up on the treasure altogether."

Izzy snatched the parchment from Dean and stared at it. Then Olly snatched it from his sister and held it up to the light. She snatched it back, then he snatched it, and they began slapping their hands at each other. Finally, Izzy pushed Olly onto the ground and sat on top of him. "Excuse my brother. Sometimes he's a total spaz."

"It's true," Olly said, out of breath.

Izzy studied the parchment and said, "Dean, I think we can help." Izzy pulled a note card from her pocket. "My friends and I recently discovered a cipher, and I think it's the same one. Ridley wrote it down for me.... Let's see if it works."

Olly and Izzy worked to decode the strange writing. Slowly, word by word, the true text began to reveal itself. "It's working!" Olly said.

"Of course it is," Izzy said with a smile.

(My dear reader, if you have not yet had a chance to use the Atbash Cipher to decode the phrases here, I recommend doing so now. It'll make this adventure far more fun.)

GL URMW GSV ULIYRWWVM,
BLF DROO SZEV GL URMW DSZG R SZEV
SRWWVM.

R SZEV TREVM BLF Z XSZMXV,
YFG ZIV BLF DROORMT GL WZMXV?

(start here)

"Dance?" Olly said. "I love to dance. But what does the fox-trot or salsa or reggaeton have to do with treasure?"

An imaginary lightbulb went off over Izzy's head. "It's a riddle. Where do people dance at the Grand Oak Resort?"

"The ballroom?" Dean asked.

"Exactly," Izzy said. "Come on."

Izzy led the others into the hotel, through the lobby, down a tall corridor, and into the Grand Oak Resort Grand Ballroom. The floors were a deep mahogany wood, and the ceiling was gilded in gold. As they walked in, the twins engaged in a short waltz that ended up with Olly tripping over his own feet. "It's like I have two right feet," he muttered.

"More like two wrong feet," Izzy chided.

The trio then checked the next part of the code.

HGZMW YVMVZGS GSV HLFIXV LU ORTSG,
MLD GFIM GL Z YRIW'H DRMGVI UORTSG.
DZOP ULIGB KZXVH GSZG DZB,

GSVM TL FK, WL MLG HGIZB.

(take 40 paces)

"This next part is confusing," Izzy said.

Olly scratched his head. "Source of light? Do you think it means that?" He pointed to the massive crystal chandelier in the center of the room.

"Eureka!" Dean said.

"Yes, I know," Olly said. "Is anyone else hungry?"

"Pastries can wait," Izzy snapped, elbowing her brother. "Focus on the task at hand. A bird's winter flight..."

"Birds fly *south*..." Olly started.

"Olly, you're a genius!" Dean said.

"...to Florida, I believe, for the daiquiris," Olly finished.

"Never mind," Dean whispered.

"Okay, we're under the chandelier and facing south. Now we walk forty paces—but how do we know how far a pace is?"

"A pace is equal to a natural step," the bellhop answered. "So about thirty inches."

"Brilliant," Olly and Izzy said. They both began

taking long strides. They followed the decoded directions and walked up the stairs of the Grand Oak Resort.

Izzy began, "Left. Okay, so the next clue suggests
we go—"

HLNV XLNV GL GSV TIZMW LZP,

ULI Z HXIFY ZMW Z HLZP.

HGZMW YVGDVVM GSV XOZDH LU GSV

YZGSRMT YVZHG,

GSVM OLLP RM GSV WRIVXGRLM PMLDM

ZH VZHG.

(walk 25 feet)

"—for a scrub and a soak. Oh, I know this one! To
the Grand Oak Spa," Olly interrupted. "But what is
the bathing beast? Do we have to fight a griffin? Or
worse, a dragon?!"

Izzy pushed past her brother. "There's no such
thing!"

"Some people say there's no such thing as magic,
but we do magic all the time."

"Illusion and stage work isn't exactly the same as mythical creatures," Izzy noted. "Come on, follow me."

"We're getting close! This is so exciting." Dean the Bellhop laughed. "I haven't had this much fun since... well, since I can't remember. Do you think we might actually find the treasure?"

"I'm certain of it," Izzy said.

The trio entered the busy spa. Women and men were walking around in plush robes and padded slippers. Some were getting manicures and pedicures while others got massages. As Olly and Izzy peeked around every corner searching for the bathing beast, some of the workers gave the children nasty looks.

"Just passing through!" Izzy said.

"Without much adieu!" Olly added.

"We'll be quick—"

"—so don't get sick."

"We'll get out of your hair—"

"—but it's only fair—"

"—to sing you a little ditty—"

"—while the spa helps you feel pretty!"

The twins broke into a short, synchronized dance. They tap-danced, their shoes clicking and clacking across the floor as they sang. When they finally stopped, everyone in the spa stood and clapped. "Thank you! Thank you!" Olly and Izzy bowed, wiping sweat from their cheeks.

"That was amazing!" Dean said.

"Just a little something I came up with," Olly said.

"If by *I*, you mean *me*, as in *I* came up with it," Izzy snorted.

"That's what I said: *I* came up with it."

Izzy and Olly glared at each other until Dean reminded them why they were there. They resumed the hunt for their treasure....

But after a few minutes, the twins started to feel deflated. "There're no animals here," Izzy whispered.

"Nope," Olly added. "The only claws I see are on that old-timey bathtub."

The three sleuths gazed at a porcelain bathtub in the corner, standing on four golden claws. "That's it!" Dean said. "But how do we stand between them?"

"Like this!" Izzy climbed into the bathtub, standing at the center. "Now we face east."

HPB ZYLEV ZMW VZIGS YVOLD,
ULOOLD GSV XOLFWH ZMW WLM'G
YV HOLD.

The three came to the end of an empty hallway. There were no doors, and only a single window.

"It's a dead end," Olly said.

"This can't be right," Izzy said.

"Did we misread one of the clues?" Dean asked. He took off his bellhop cap and scratched his head.

Izzy and Olly read the last decoded clue out loud. "Follow the clouds...." They looked outside the window. The clouds were up...so the twins both looked up at the ceiling off the hallway. An almost unnoticeable square was overhead. "The attic!"

Dean reached up and found the cord to pull down the attic stairs. The three quickly climbed the ladder and entered the loft space at the top of the resort. The massive room ran the entire length of the hotel. It was a place used as storage. There were hundreds, maybe thousands—maybe tens of thousands—of items: chairs, tables, dishware, silverware, furniture, taxidermy, lost luggage, trunks, sheets, towels, seasonal decorations, and more.

"This place is a hotel museum! How are we supposed to find something in this mess?!" Olly whined. "Going over every inch of this place would take decades!"

"Read the last line," Izzy suggested to her brother.

"As clever as a fox," Olly said.

"How are foxes clever?"

"I haven't the foggiest idea...."

"Don't they hide in holes?"

"How do we find a hole in a space as big as this?!"

The twins didn't know where to begin. They started searching, but after an hour, they started to give up hope. Even Dean the bellhop began to slouch. "This has been fun, but I suppose I should really get back to work before I get in trouble."

"No. Don't give up," Izzy said. "We've made it this far. We'll find your treasure."

"Yeah. What she said," Olly agreed. "We're not the brightest kids around—"

"Speak for yourself," Izzy interjected.

"—but we're plenty clever. We make foxes look... well, not clever."

"Do we?" Izzy asked.

"We do," Olly concluded. He pointed at a taxidermy

fox on a nearby mantle. "See? If that fox was so clever, how come it got killed and stuffed?"

Izzy froze. She whispered, "It's a fox."

"Clearly," Olly said with a roll of his eyes.

"No, it's a *fox*," Izzy said, pushing past her twin brother.

"So?" Olly said, before it finally dawned on him. They were looking at their final clue. "Oh!"

The twins rushed over. Together, they pulled on the mantelpiece, and a secret compartment slid out, revealing a hole in the wall. Inside was a box. Dean pulled the box out and rolled it over in his hands. "It's just a box?"

"It's not just any box," Olly said. "It's a puzzle box. Like the one Leila found."

"And the one Carter inherited from his dad," Izzy added.

"Do you think it's related to those?" Olly asked. "Do you think it belonged to another member of the Emerald Ring?"

"It has to be. It looks just like them," Izzy said.

"What's an Emerald Ring?" Dean asked, confused.

"It's a group of kid magicians, like us Misfits, but from thirty years ago."

"So wait," Dean moaned, flustered, "you're telling me this isn't a treasure at all? It's just some box a kid left here three decades ago? I've been searching for this treasure for years, and it's just a....a...children's game?!"

"What's wrong with children?" Olly asked.

"It might still have treasure inside," Izzy noted.

"Ha! Unlikely!" Dean shouted. He yanked off his hat and squeezed it with agitation. "Whatever's inside, you kids can have it. I'm going back to work." And with that, the bellhop stormed out of the attic.

The twins shrugged. "Another mystery solved," Olly said.

"And another mystery presents itself," Izzy added. "What do you think is inside?"

"Who knows? The point is, we had an adventure. And a fun one. Time for a nap?"

"I hate naps," Izzy said.

"I love naps," Olly said.

"Are you certain we're related?"

"Not at all."

"Obviously. I mean, I got all the good looks."

"Ha! Wrong again."

The twins continued their banter as they returned

to their room with their newfound prize. Little did they know that a pair of eyes watched them from the shadows as a sinister and sly smile crept over Dean's face. "Yes, that worked out perfectly," Dean whispered. "Everything is falling into place...."